Jacqui Davey

Sweaters Without Borders

A simple hobby can reach across the globe

novum pro

www.novum-publishing.co.uk

All rights of distribution, including via film, radio, and television, photomechanical reproduction, audio storage media, electronic data storage media, and the reprinting of portions of text, are reserved.

Printed in the European Union on environmentally friendly, chlorine- and acid-free paper.

© 2020 novum publishing

ISBN 978-3-99064-869-8
Editing: Ashleigh Brassfield, DipEdit
Cover photos: Patrick Guenette, Antoniosantosg | Dreamstime.com
Cover design, layout & typesetting: novum publishing

www.novum-publishing.co.uk

CONTENTS

YOUNG JENNY

"Hurry up, Jenny! We need to leave now in case we're stuck in a bomb scare. You know Auntie Sue's plane flies at four o'clock!" Vicky shouted to Jenny, her daughter.

"I'm coming!" Jenny replied, as she quickly rushed down the stairs and out the front door, carrying Auntie Sue's large brown suitcase in one hand and her small red bag in the other. Jenny threw the little red bag into the boot of her Mum's turquoise Mini, then jumped into the back seat and squeezed the large brown suitcase in beside her. As Vicky started the engine, Jenny leaned forward and spoke to Auntie Sue, who was already in the front passenger seat. "I wish I was going with you to Vietnam! I'd love to see the faces of the little children who get your sweaters, just like the wee kids in Africa that you showed me in your photos."

Sue wasn't long back from a place called Biafra, in Africa, where there'd also been trouble, but now she was travelling as a nurse to a clinic in Vietnam to treat people who'd been injured in the recent war. There'd been a programme about Vietnam on TV the evening before and Miss Young, Jenny's geography teacher, had talked about it in class. Sue normally worked in the Accident and Emergency Department of the Belfast City Hospital, but every six months she volunteered as a nurse for a large overseas charity. Jenny thought Auntie Sue was cool, because she loved to help others and even looked a bit like herself!

As Jenny tried to make herself comfortable in the backseat, she asked another question. "Auntie Sue, how many sweaters have you got in your little red bag this time?"

Sue smiled as she replied, "I've lost count, but I think there's about thirty. No doubt I'll meet children in desperate need of new clothes."

"I'm sure those children will like them," Jenny said. "I wish I could knit. I still haven't got the hang of it, and I even find it hard to wrap the wool around my needles. Miss Kershaw, our craft teacher, is always cross and thinks I'm the worst knitter ever! At least it'll be the summer holidays in a couple of weeks, and I'll get away from her for a while!"

"Don't worry," Sue said in response. "I'm only away for six weeks this time, but I promise I'll help you when I get back. I've never been to Vietnam before and I guess I'm going to be busy treating lots of injured patients or helping orphaned kids."

Jenny felt sorry for children like that, and she said, "I saw a photograph of a wee Vietnamese girl in the Belfast Telegraph with terrible burns on her skin; I hope she gets better quickly. I know you might meet patients like her. There's two boys in my class from Vietnam and they've both got lovely shiny black hair."

A few moments later, Jenny straightened up and looked out the window as she realized they'd reached the Ormeau Bridge, about a mile away from Newtownbreda, where they'd started. As Vicky manoeuvred her car into the inner city bound lane over the Bridge, Jenny exclaimed, "Hey, look at those rowing boats in the river! They're going really fast!"

Auntie Sue responded, "They're probably students from Queens' University Boat Club. They must be pretty fit, they're travelling at some speed!" Jenny nodded in agreement.

The car suddenly shuddered as Vicky put her foot on the brake and exclaimed, "Oh no! I don't think we're going anywhere fast! There's a huge traffic jam ahead!"

Normally it took an hour to get to the airport from Newtownbreda, but it would be an awful lot longer with a road-block. Jenny could make out an army jeep on the bridge as Vicky switched off the ignition and turned to Sue. "We might not make it in time for your flight, Sis. We'll just have to wait it out in this queue."

This worried Jenny, as she didn't want Auntie Sue missing her flight to London, nor her onward connection from Heathrow Airport to Vietnam.

Vicky turned on the car radio just as a newsflash came over the airwaves. "Oh no," she quietly muttered. "A bomb's gone off in the city centre. That must have been the bang I heard before leaving the house." Jenny had also heard a bang while she was in the bathroom, and it was likely to have been the same one.

Just then the sound of a fire brigade reached them from the other side of the bridge. "That must be the firefighters trying to get to the bomb site; they're very brave. Ricky told me he wants to be a firefighter someday," Jenny said to her mother and aunt.

"That wee brother of yours can hardly climb the ladder to his bunk bed, he'd certainly not manage a ladder that needs to stretch to the top of high buildings," Vicky added as she shook her head. "I just wish he'd put his head down and do a bit more homework, instead of rushing off to play football all the time!" Jenny had to agree. Ricky wasn't too bad as a brother, and he'd often let her share his sweeties, which he bought on the way home from school on Fridays.

Gradually, the cars started to move, but it took about ten minutes before Vicky's small car reached the front of the queue.

At this stage, a young soldier stepped over to the car, fixing his gaze on the brown suitcase in the rear seat. "Your driving licence, please, Ma'am," he requested of Vicky, as he bent his head through the driver's window. Jenny thought his voice sounded very like the new P5 teacher at school, who'd recently come from England, and he looked about the same age.

The soldier quickly glanced at Vicky's licence as another taller and older-looking soldier emerged from the nearby jeep and approached the car. It was easy to spot a scar above his right eyebrow, as he hadn't much hair. "Please open your car doors and unlock the boot," he abruptly requested. "A vehicle search is required."

Sue now started to look panicky, as time really wasn't on her side and she needed to get to the airport. "Please, could you be quick?" Vicky asked anxiously. "We're in a hurry as my sister's heading off to Vietnam and needs to catch a four o'clock connecting flight to London from Aldergrove Airport."

The older soldier didn't reply as he signalled the younger recruit to step back and started a search of the car. He opened the boot, checked under the seats and glanced into the compartment under the dashboard. He then lifted Sue's small red bag from the boot and peeked at the contents. "I guess you're taking these with you," he addressed Sue.

"Yes," Sue replied. "I plan to give them out to kids at a Clinic where I'll be working." The soldier placed the bag back into the boot then spoke again. "Be careful of landmines in the villages, Ma'am. I'm not long back from a tour of duty there myself. Avoid the city centre and aim for the M2." The two soldiers then waved the next car forward as Vicky started up the car again and headed for the northbound motorway, not taking long to bypass the city centre.

Sue turned around to Jenny while she gazed out the window at Cavehill Mountain and Belfast Lough and asked, "Do you know that landmark over there?"

Jenny nodded, "It's the Belfast shipyard, where the famous Titanic ship was built, and it sunk after it hit an iceberg on its very first voyage."

"You're right, Jenny," Sue responded. "Belfast Shipyard has turned out several fine ships and cruise liners, but the Titanic is probably the most famous one."

As Aunt Sue and Jenny continued to chat, Vicky kept her foot on the accelerator and drove as fast as she could within the speed limits, bearing in mind she'd three bodies and Auntie Sue's baggage on board! About twenty minutes later an airport exit sign appeared up ahead.

"I'm glad we're nearly there!" Jenny moaned from the back seat, as she was now feeling cramped and sore. "I've got pins and needles all over! That's what I get for being squashed beside your big suitcase, Auntie Sue!"

Auntie Sue gave a small laugh as Vicky turned off the M2 motorway and drove towards the A57 junction, which showed a sign for the airport six miles further on.

Vicky drove on about another three miles until Sue suddenly blurted out, "Oh no! I think there's another security checkpoint coming up! I forgot about this one! It'll be a miracle if I ever get my London flight!"

Vicky slowed up before the checkpoint as a security guard quickly stepped forward and waved her on. "Maybe that Vietnam veteran warned him we were coming!" she said with a chuckle as Vicky and Jenny nodded. The last thing Sue needed now was to get stuck in another queue.

Without further delay, Vicky kept going and soon spotted Aldergrove Airport up ahead. It didn't take long to go through the entrance and head for the short-stay car park where Jenny quickly spotted a parking space. This meant they'd now caught up, timewise, and Sue could connect with her flight after all.

Vicky turned to Sue and quietly spoke as she switched off the engine. "Jenny and I will stay for a wee while to see your plane off, so I'll lock the car and we can walk over to the terminal together."

"That'll be great," Sue replied. "I'm going to miss you guys, but I'll try and phone if I get a connection." Vicky and Jenny got out of the car first and helped Sue to lift her suitcase and little red bag onto a trolley, then the three of them took it in turns to push the trolley across the car park to the terminal building. When they got to the Departures entrance Vicky and Jenny could go no further.

"We'll hang around for a bit in the main terminal," Vicky said. "I know Jenny wants to see your plane taking off, and you can give us a wave from the runway!"

Sue gave both of them a hug as a small tear rolled down her cheek. "I'll make sure my little red bag is on board," she said with a slight giggle." I don't want to leave my little sweaters behind!" Sue then headed for check-in, as Vicky and Sue went off to find the airport viewing area.

It didn't take long for Vicky and Jenny to spot an upstairs café with a few vacant tables overlooking the runway, and they decided to order a snack.

Jenny asked, "Mum, can I have a packet of sandwiches and a Fanta orange? I'm a bit hungry, but I don't want you to spend too much."

Vicky replied, "That's okay, Jen. I'm glad you noticed the airport prices are on the expensive side, but I'm a bit peckish myself, so I'll order the same." Jenny found and guarded a table while Vicky walked over to the food counter to place their order. It took several minutes for Vicky to come back, as there'd been a long queue.

"Oh great! You've picked my favourite!" Jenny exclaimed as Vicky lifted two packets of sandwiches and two cans of orange Fanta from the tray in her hand and placed them onto the table. "Can I swop one of my egg and onion sandwiches for one of your ham and cheese ones?" Jenny asked as Vicky unwrapped the sandwiches and pulled the rings off the top of the Fanta cans.

"Go ahead. These will have to keep us going until teatime, and we could face another bomb scare on the way home."

Jenny really hoped not, and decided to enjoy her snack, as they'd at least got Auntie Sue safely to the airport and on time! Suddenly, there was an announcement.

"This is the last call for all British European Airways passengers travelling to London Heathrow on Flight BEA 1214. Please proceed to gate 5."

Jenny turned to Vicky. "Hey Mum, that's Auntie Sue's flight! Her plane will be going in a few minutes." Jenny sucked the last dregs of her Fanta through a straw while Vicky gave her a nudge.

"Look, Jenny! There's the baggage going onto that plane over there."

Jenny looked up and saw a huge pile of suitcases and bags being loaded off a small truck onto a large plane that stood on the runway. She couldn't help noticing a small red bag being transferred into the hold at the rear of aircraft.

"Look, that's Auntie Sue little red bag, the one with her small knitted sweaters inside!" Jenny proclaimed. "I hope all the Vietnamese children who need one get one!"

"I hope so too," commented Vicky. "It's lovely our Sue's able to knit, and she'll be able to help you when she gets back! She might even show you how to make a little sweater!"

"That would be cool!" responded Jenny." I told her about Miss Kershaw's awful craft classes on Monday afternoons, and how she's always cross with me since I'm hopeless at knitting!"

Miss Kershaw's craft class was quickly forgotten as Jenny and Vicky watched the British European Airways plane preparing to leave. Within a few minutes, the aircraft doors were closed, the passenger steps were moved away, and the huge propellers began to rotate on the wings. The propellers then got faster as the aircraft slowly reversed, turned ninety degrees, and headed towards the runway, disappearing from sight. Jenny and Vicky set their empty Fanta bottles and rubbish onto their tray then stood up to get a clearer view out the window.

"I wish I was on Auntie Sue's flight," Jenny said quietly.

Vicky smiled softly as she turned towards Jenny in response. "Maybe someday you'll go off on an aircraft yourself, but I think Sue will have plenty to do in Vietnam without us around! Her plane should be coming back into view any moment!"

Suddenly, there was a huge rumbling noise and the plane reappeared. Jenny couldn't take her eyes off the huge aircraft as it sped up the runway like a large silver bird roaring into the sky. At last, Auntie Sue was on her way to Vietnam! Jenny couldn't wait to hear her stories on her return! Maybe someday she'd become a nurse herself, or go off to an overseas country! But for now, she desperately needed to learn how to knit: there was still Miss Kershaw's craft class to cope with on Monday afternoon.

Monday afternoon soon arrived…

Jenny couldn't help thinking about her Aunt as she gazed out of the P6 classroom window, spotting a few seagulls and a helicopter overhead. "I wonder what Auntie Sue's doing in Vietnam at the moment. I hope she's not too busy or tired." At that moment, Jenny was quickly brought back to the present as Miss Kershaw was approaching, inspecting each pupil's knitting on her way around the classroom. "You're not my favourite teacher, and I don't like your black rimmed glasses at the end of your nose!" Jenny muttered to herself, as Miss Kershaw got dangerously close. She also didn't like the way her dark brown hair was pinned like a beehive on the top of her head!

Just then, Jenny glanced down. "Oh no, I've done it again!" she gasped. "I've dropped another stitch!" She'd been attempting to knit a long maxi scarf, but the piece of woolly cloth hanging off the end of her two wooden needles wasn't exactly a work of art! She'd already dropped five stitches and the colour was a horrible mustard shade. Jenny hadn't wanted to knit anything that colour, but it had been the only cheap and cheerful chunky wool that Vicky could find in the local wool shop. "I wish I could master the basic stitches in the pattern and not feel so clumsy," Jenny thought. "It's hard making something long enough to stretch around my neck without a lot of holes in it!"

Thankfully, the bell suddenly rang before Miss Kershaw got any further! "Great! I didn't realise it was that late. At least Miss Kershaw won't see my mistakes now," Jenny mumbled to herself as she quickly finished the row she'd been knitting and stuffed her work into a large paper bag. She was ashamed of her so-called "scarf." It was a much bigger challenge than she'd first thought! Most of her other classmates were producing beautiful pieces of work, like stripy tea cosies or gloves. Even Carole, her best friend, had already finished lots of small coloured squares to make into a colourful patchwork blanket. Jenny just wanted to make something to be proud of, and to let Miss Kershaw see that she really did have some talent! Roll on, Auntie Sue's return!

CHAPTER ONE

TWENTY YEARS ON

Jenny woke up with a jolt and yawned before glancing down at her mobile phone and got a bit of a shock. "Oh no!" she gasped. "I can't believe it's six o'clock. No wonder I've a sore neck! I must have been asleep for over three hours!"

Poor Jenny's head had been squashed against the edge of the sofa for most of the afternoon, so it was no wonder she felt uncomfortable! She also realized she'd been dreaming! It was hard to recall all the details, but part of the dream had been watching a large plane taking off from Aldergrove Airport on a nice summer day with Auntie Sue on board. Another part of it was about several small children sitting outside a small wooden dwelling, wearing little red sweaters. All of them had shining black hair and looked as if they came from a country in Asia. Jenny knew this dream reminded her of Auntie Sue going off on her volunteering trip to Vietnam as a nurse. Now, twenty years later, Jenny was a district nurse herself!

"Life was a lot simpler then." Jenny quietly muttered. "My biggest challenges in those days were doing maths homework or trying to knit a scarf in Miss Kershaw's craft class! Now I've lots of patients to treat! I needed that doze this afternoon, after two evening shifts this week!"

Jenny gave herself a long stretch then decided to go and get fed. Lunch was a long while back and a few hunger pangs were starting!

As Jenny got up from the sofa, she lifted the TV remote control from the coffee table in front of her and pressed the keypad for ITV. It was good timing as a news headline had just started on the screen:

A low-flying helicopter seemed to be circling over a young female reporter's head as she stood in front of a barren landscape in intense heat with bony-ribbed cows and a struggling mass of people walking behind her. Many of the small, bloated-bellied children looked frightened or displayed vacant stares. There didn't seem to be many older people in the crowd, but several young women carried babies on their backs.

Jenny caught the end of the young reporter's speech:

"… this year's harvest has failed, and hundreds are arriving daily at this refugee camp, walking over 100 kilometres to get emergency food aid. There's been no rain for fifteen months and temperatures have now reached forty degrees centigrade, even in the shade. 5 million people are at risk of starvation. Hunger will steal their futures and, without support from other countries, many of these refugees will starve. This is Trish Flanagan from ITN, reporting from Juba in Sudan."

As Trish's voice tailed off, Jenny saw a small girl standing in the foreground of the TV screen alongside an adult and younger child. She could hardly stand up straight and looked extremely frail, with sagging dull skin around her neck and ankles. A few moments later the little girl appeared to collapse to the ground. The adult, who was likely her mother, quickly bent over to pick her up, but could barely reach down to ground level herself as she also looked weak and exhausted. Someone walked past a few moments later and seemed to step on the little girl's hand. Jenny noticed her small face grimacing in pain, but no one seemed to be aware of this except her mother, as her gentle cries for help were too faint to be heard in the crowd.

As the news report ended, Jenny noticed aid workers handing out blankets, small garments and food rations from large cardboard boxes to several queues of waiting people. A request then followed on the screen for money to be sent to a charity appeal. Jenny thought to herself, "I must send in a donation, but I don't know what else I could do right now." The image of the little girl stuck in her mind as she switched the TV off and headed to the kitchen to grab something to eat.

As Jenny walked over to the fridge to lift out some salad vegetables and the remains of a Domino's Pizza from the evening before, she glanced sideways at a small wall-mounted frame nearby. It displayed a newspaper cutting of a young man wearing a firefighter's uniform, standing proudly in front of a large fire engine with a helmet in his hand. He looked strong and handsome, with bright blue eyes and cropped dark hair. Jenny felt a few tears on her cheek as she closed the fridge door and quietly whispered towards the frame, "Steve, I wish you'd not been on duty the night the fire broke out in Reaville Tower. Being married to you for two years wasn't long enough!" Jenny wasn't the only one who'd become a widow that evening. She hadn't forgotten the phone call from Steve's fire station that had changed her world forever...

Steve should have been home at eleven o'clock, and normally phoned Jenny if he was going to be late, but that evening he hadn't. When the phone eventually rang at about one o'clock in the morning, Jenny ran to answer it, hearing the voice of Steve's Fire Station Commander, Rodney Smith, at the other end.

"Jenny, there's been an incident at a multi-storey building in the city centre tonight. Four of our station crews were sent out as the fire rapidly spread and a number of rescues attempted, but sadly some of the guys got hurt." Rodney then took a deep breath and continued, "Jenny, I know this is difficult to hear, but Steve's one of the injured. He's been taken to the Accident and Emergency Department at the Royal Victoria Hospital, and he's in pretty bad shape."

Jenny hadn't heard the rest of the conversation as she'd dashed outside to her Fiat and headed straight to the hospital. When she'd got there, several firefighters from Blue Watch and a number of rescued multi-storey tower residents had already arrived, all suffering from burns or smoke inhalation. Deputy Fire Station Manager Paul Osborne had appeared a short time later and quietly ushered Jenny into a small office to meet a kindly young doctor with a tired, pale face. The young doctor had spoken slowly and thoughtfully as he addressed Jenny.

"I'm really sorry to share this news, Mrs O'Neill. My colleagues in A&E did everything possible to save your husband. He sustained third degree burns to over 75% of his body plus additional lung damage from smoke. Sadly, we've lost him."

Jenny had been in total shock. Steve was only 28 years old and had the rest of his life in front of him. He was rarely sick, had often run marathons and even trained with the local Mountain Rescue Team on a regular basis. He'd also been great at DIY jobs. Jenny didn't know what she'd do without him.

That had been eighteen months ago, and life had moved on, but Jenny often felt it hadn't.

Jenny lifted her re-heated pizza out of the microwave as more tears started to flow. Losing Steve had been like losing her right arm, and she was still trying to come to grips with the rest of her life. Maybe she needed to focus on a new beginning, maybe something like a simple new hobby. The thought of the little injured girl in the news report from Sudan also kept coming to mind...

After finishing her pizza and salad, Jenny decided to do something she'd been putting off for a very long time, going up to the attic to sort more of Steve's items for giving away. She'd avoided this as long as possible, but tonight she'd nothing else planned.

As she stacked her used dishes into the dishwasher beside the backdoor, Jenny felt a bit guilty, as she really no longer needed the machine, now that she lived on her own. It had been handy when Steve was around but perhaps it was now time to pass it onto someone else with a lot more mouths to feed. Jenny closed the dishwasher door, set the control, then headed to the attic to sort more of Steve's stuff.

After climbing up the thin wooden staircase from the landing, Jenny quickly spotted a large brown box in one corner of the attic, covered in a thick layer of dust. She walked over and gently opened the lid, exposing some old medals and trophies Steve had won in Fire Service sporting events. She also came across an old yellow bin bag, containing some of Steve's old shirts and a pair of swimming trunks that he'd worn at a charity swimming gala in the Ormeau Baths. Several more bags and large boxes were stacked up, filled with items that had been put away just after Steve's death. As Jenny gently lifted items from the bags and boxes and placed them into a pile for further sorting, she muttered to herself, "I wish I wasn't so tired. I'll have another look at these tomorrow when I'm not so exhausted."

As she began to walk towards the attic ladder to return downstairs, Jenny spotted another small red bag in a corner. She walked over to pick it up, brushed the dust off its surface and opened the flap at the top. It wasn't heavy and there seemed to be a piece of paper and something like sticks inside. Jenny slowly pulled out the contents...

A pair of knitting needles, a small measuring tape and a well-thumbed pattern for a child's sweater emerged. The pattern was in three sizes and looked quite easy, including plain and purl stitches and with small sleeves sewn into the sides. Jenny remembered attempting plain and purl stitches in Miss Kershaw's class many years before! She also noticed Auntie Sue's delicate handwriting on parts of the pattern. In recent years Sue hadn't been able to write clearly, as she'd been ill and sadly died from cancer not long after she'd gone to work in England. Jenny also pulled out a small coloured postcard from the bag with a map of Vietnam on the front. This bag must be the one she'd seen Auntie Sue taking on her Vietnamese trip, and Jenny remembered the stories she'd shared on her return, especially about the kids who'd received one of her little sweaters, like the one on the pattern in Jenny's hand now.

As Jenny climbed back down the ladder, still grasping the pattern in her hand, a small idea started to form in her head. She could try to knit a little sweater from Auntie Sue's old pattern. The needles in the bag were the correct size and she'd just need to get a couple of balls of nice wool.

"I'll go into town tomorrow and buy some wool," Jenny thought to herself. "I've some shopping to do anyway, and a plan to meet Carole for lunch when I'm there."

A short while later, Jenny decided it was time for an early night. As she got ready for bed, she couldn't help thinking about the little famine-stricken girl in the ITV news report. "I wonder if anyone will offer her a nice warm sweater?" she asked herself. She was still trying to answer that question as she slipped into bed and slowly drifted off to sleep.

CHAPTER TWO

INTO TOWN

"I just adore autumn," Jenny thought to herself as she looked at the changing colours of the leaves on the trees through the bus window, heading along the Lisburn Road towards the Belfast city centre. She sighed with relief as she glanced at her watch. "At least it's only 10.30 am, but I'd better not be late. It's not every-day Carole's free to meet me on a Saturday morning."

Jenny and Carole had been best friends since their school-days, and regularly made time to meet up for a chat. Carole had also given Jenny lots of practical support and a listening ear af-ter Steve's death.

"These roadworks never seem to stop," Jenny thought as she glanced out the window again. There had been lots of repairs to the roads over the previous year, including the installation of new phone lines and underground water pipes.

At the next junction there seemed to be a small traffic jam, close to Reaville Tower, where Steve had died, but it quickly cleared.

About eight minutes later the bus reached Donegall Square East, a bit quicker than Jenny expected. She'd got fifteen minutes to spare before meeting Carole, so she decided to take a brisk walk around the shops. Near the new Law Courts building, there was an interesting display in the window of a little craft shop at the back of Littlewoods store. Jenny remembered visiting this place in the past with Auntie Sue, when she'd popped in to buy some wool before heading off on some of her overseas charity trips. Vicky had also popped into the shop to buy buttons for Ricky's school uniforms, and it was hard to believe that he was now a schoolteacher himself.

After spending a few moments glancing at a selection of pret-ty knitted toys in the window, Jenny decided to enter the shop, nearly falling over a large basket of brightly coloured wool on the floor beside the door. On an opposite wall hung a huge sign which read, "20% discount off all items!" Jenny mumbled to herself, "That's not a bad bargain!" as she gazed at a range of pretty knitted scarves, small motifs, buttons of about every colour you could think of and, of course, the items in the window.

Jenny bent down to lift a couple of balls of red wool from the basket at the door and gently squeezed them in her hand. They were nice and soft to touch, and their red colour looked warm and bright. She quickly decided to buy several of them as the wool was not only pretty but also double knitting, the correct weight of wool needed to make a small garment from Auntie Sue's pattern. "I'm definitely going to have a go at making a wee sweater, even though it's a lot harder than making a scarf," Jenny pondered to herself. "I might have been a pretty awful knitter in Miss Kershaw's craft class at school, but I did improve later with Auntie Sue's tuition!"

A sales assistant, who was standing behind a counter on the far side of the shop, putting knitting patterns into folders, smiled at Jenny and said, "That wool you're holding is on special offer this week. Each 100g ball is normally £3.99, but they're only £2.50 each at the moment."

Jenny made a brief calculation in her head: 2 balls would cost £5.00: another 2 balls would only cost £10.00. Before she changed her mind, she decided to buy 4 balls of the wool and dipped into her handbag to lift a £10.00 pound note from her purse.

As Jenny handed over the cash, the sales assistant asked her, "What are you planning to make?" Jenny told her about the child's sweater pattern that she'd found in the attic the evening before and how she wanted to try knitting one. "That's a great idea," the young sales assistant responded. "If it turned out half decent, you could even make another! At least you'll have enough wool!" Jenny had to agree.

As the sales assistant packed the red balls of wool into a brown paper bag and wrote out a receipt, Jenny glanced again at her watch and said, "I'd better get a move on. I've to meet a friend at The Skandia Cafe in about five minutes. She'll be wondering where I am if I'm late."

The young assistant quickly responded, "No problem. I'd better let you get away. I hope your little sweater turns out okay!" Jenny then gave a short wave and muttered some thanks as she picked up her bag of purchased wool and walked out the shop door. She then headed for Great Victoria Street, walking past the YMCA, H Samuel Jewellers and the Car Tax office, before reaching the block of buildings that housed The Skandia Café.

Jenny quickly spotted Carole staring out of one of the café windows that overlooked the back of the City Hall, one of Belfast's most beautiful historical buildings. Jenny entered the door of the café and quickly walked towards the table where Carole was seated with a menu in her hand. Carole pushed back the table to let Jenny squeeze into a seat, as she uttered, "I hope you haven't been working too hard, Jenny. It's time you took a bit of a break and gave yourself a rest. Why not sit down and order yourself a wee treat? I can assure you this menu's got a great choice to pick from!"

Jenny let her bags sink to the floor, took off her jacket, then sat down before picking up a small printed menu from the table. "It's not too hard to guess what I'm going to order! My favourites are on the list, chocolate muffins and Americano coffee. Even though I've recently put on a few pounds, I'm going to spoil myself this morning!"

"That's the spirit!" Carole responded. "I'll order the same myself! I know there's also a nice selection of scones and tray bakes, but the muffins in here are about the best you'll find in Belfast!" This made Jenny chuckle slightly and made her feel less guilty about her choice. As Carole got up to place their order, Jenny spotted a selection of daily newspapers in a small wall rack behind her. As she stretched over to the rack and lifted out a copy of the Daily Mail, placing it on the table, she couldn't help noticing the main topic on the front page: it was a picture of the Sudanese refugee camp on the news the night before, displaying several photographs of small children and babies, including one that looked very like the little girl in the previous evening's report. Underneath the photographs was a contact phone number and address for charity donations. Jenny lifted a small notebook and pen from her handbag and wrote the details down, as she still planned to forward some money to the appeal. A few moments later, Carole returned to the table and their chat resumed.

Carole spoke first. "Jenny, I can't believe it's nearly twenty years since we sat together in school. I always knew you were going to end up as a nurse like your Auntie Sue. I remember visiting your folks one evening when Sue arrived for a meal after a day's shift at the Belfast City Hospital. Your Mum had made a gorgeous corned beef pie and your brother Ricky certainly wasn't slow in trying to get a large portion of it!" Jenny laughed: she remembered that evening herself! Ricky had always loved to show off when visitors came for a meal. After chatting a bit more about family, Jenny changed the subject.

"Carole, do you remember when I tried to knit a scarf in Miss Kershaw's class?"

Carole smiled and gave a small cough. "I remember your scarf only too well, and especially the day it was caught in the school bus doors! How could anyone forget Miss Kershaw! She was always cross with our class, since we were all slow knitters, and she gave you a particularly hard time, Jenny! If I remember correctly, I made a patchwork blanket and a pair of socks for my Dad in her class." Jenny knew this was correct. Carole had always been a much better knitter than herself and had made several nice things.

After chatting a bit more, Carole spoke again. "Do you know something, Jenny? You've always stood with me in the good times and bad, even when I didn't do very well in my A Levels and wasn't sure what to do next. I hope we'll still be friends when we're ninety, if we're both around that long!"

It was Jenny's turn to smile. "I hope so too, Carole. You've been a real friend yourself through thick and thin. I even remember you lending me your platform shoes when we went to school discos!" This image got them both giggling. Carole always managed to say the right words to cheer Jenny up, especially since Steve's death.

"Apart from yourself, Carole, what about that young niece of yours?" Jenny asked. "What's she doing at the moment?"

Carole replied, "Oh, you mean Tracey? She's just finishing the third year of her medical course at Queens University. She'd often thought of doing nursing after admiring your Auntie Sue, but was great at science subjects and pretty smart, so she decided to do medicine instead. She's about to head off to Africa for six weeks to do a medical elective – that's the part of her training where she's to practice being a doctor in the real world. She's going to work in a clinic at a Refugee Camp in Sudan, which I know was on the news this week." Jenny was delighted to hear that. "In fact," Carole continued, "Tracey's packed about every size of bandage you could think of into her suitcase, not to mention insect repellent and lots of other small medical supplies."

Jenny was impressed with Tracey's plans. She knew she was a bright girl with a caring heart towards others, and not surprised she'd chosen to train as a doctor.

Jenny thought for a moment before speaking again. "I'd like to give Tracey something to take to Africa that might help one of her patients. I'm thinking about knitting a small child's sweater from an old pattern of Auntie Sue's, and I'll pass it on if it ever gets completed."

"That's kind of you," Carole responded. "Tracey would be glad of any support."

Whilst Carole and Jenny waited for their coffee and muffins to be served, Carole couldn't help noticing Jenny looked a lot more relaxed and less tired since their previous get-together in August.

She also spotted a ball of red wool hanging out of one of Jenny's shopping bags. This prompted her to speak again. "Jenny, I've just had a sudden thought. As you're an aspiring knitter, I wonder if you'd be free on Tuesday night? I've recently joined a wee craft class that meets once a fortnight in the Library beside the Ormeau Bridge, with a motley crew including everything from seventeen years old to well over seventy! Some produce works of art whilst others just knit and natter! Why don't you come next week if you're not working? I could pick you up around 7.15pm as the class starts at 7.30pm. You'll get a free cup of coffee if you manage to stick the first hour!"

Jenny had to admit this could be worth a try. "OK, Carole," she replied. "It sounds fun! I'll be ready for collection at 7.15pm on Tuesday! I'll also bring some knitting!"

A young waitress then arrived with coffee and muffins, which were soon demolished, as Jenny and Carole agreed the muffins were delicious and the coffee tasted great. The waitress even came back and refilled their cups!

Soon they realised it was nearly lunchtime and time to get going. Jenny and Carole both needed to complete some shopping before heading home, so confirmed arrangements for the following Tuesday evening. As they prepared to leave, Jenny and Carole both placed a small tip on the table before making a bee line for the Café's front door.

"See you about seven o'clock on Tuesday!" shouted Carole, as she headed to the Europa Hotel car park to collect her car, whilst Jenny aimed for Marks and Spencer to buy a couple of ready meals and some bread. She thought it would be nice to invite Carole around for tea some evening to thank her for her recent kindness and support.

After completing her shopping, Jenny arrived at the bus stop, just as the Number 9 Finaghy bus pulled up. A teenage boy who was already in the queue stepped onto the vehicle first, followed by Jenny, who handed a one-pound coin to the driver as her fare.

"I see you've been busy shopping," the driver said, as he passed her a ticket. "You'll be glad to get home and put your feet up!" Jenny nodded in reply, as she grabbed her bags and headed for the upper deck, not an easy feat with her Marks and Spencer groceries in one hand and a bag full of wool in the other! After reaching the top of the stairs, Jenny spotted a free double seat near the front of the bus so quickly walked over to it and sat down, placing her bags of purchases onto the seat beside her. At least she'd a great vantage point from the top deck!

As the bus trundled along towards Finaghy, Jenny couldn't help thinking about the wool she'd just bought and her plans to make a small child's sweater. It would be a nice little project to try, as it wasn't too hard and had only a few instructions. "I'll make a start later on," Jenny muttered to herself, as she stretched out her legs to make herself more comfortable. About twenty minutes later and without significant hassle, she arrived safely home, getting off the bus just a short distance from her own street.

After opening the front door, Jenny headed for the kitchen, where she set her bags down on the worktop and put her groceries into the fridge. She then opened the paper bag with the balls of wool inside before running upstairs to the attic, where she quickly located Auntie Sue's small red knitting bag and brought it downstairs.

A few moments later, after sitting down at the kitchen table and opening Auntie Sue's bag, Jenny lifted out the small child's sweater pattern, the pair of needles and small measuring tape. She then walked over to the cutlery drawer under the sink and fetched a pair of kitchen scissors before returning to the table, where it didn't take her long to unravel some wool and cast on fifty four stitches, the recommended number for a four or five year old child's sweater. In a very short time, she'd knitted several rows of plain and purl stitches, called stocking stitch, before deciding to take a short break. The woolly cloth was now about ten centimetres long.

"Gosh, I think I'd better stop, my fingers are starting to get sore," Jenny mumbled to herself, as she set down her knitting and made her way to the living room to switch on the TV for the ITV news, just as she'd done the evening before.

It didn't take long for an updated report to come onto the screen about the Sudanese refugee camp in Juba. The same reporter, Trish Flanagan, was giving an updated summary of the famine relief work in the camp that day...

"More and more refugees arrived this morning, many dying from hunger or weak with exhaustion after walking many miles under baking hot sun."

As Trish spoke, Jenny could make out several nurses, doctors and aid workers in the background and thought of Tracey, who was going to Sudan in a few days' time. As the news report ended, Jenny's eyes started to brim with tears. She was sad for the people in the Refugee Camp and felt helpless about doing much to aid their suffering, but still planned to make a financial donation.

As she turned off the TV and headed back to the kitchen to resume her knitting, Jenny remembered what the sales assistant had suggested in the craft shop, "If your small sweater turns out alright, you could donate it to a good cause." Jenny decided she'd definitely donate her finished sweater to Tracey to take on her medical elective if it turned out in any way decent.

In roughly two hours, Jenny managed to complete the back of the small garment, with a further plan to knit the front and sleeves in the next few days. She then placed the small piece of knitting into Auntie Sue's old knitting bag, for storage in a cupboard in the back bedroom. It would be ready for "further action" when she resumed her small "project" again, most likely at the knitting workshop on Tuesday, if she wasn't on duty that night!

CHAPTER THREE

AT THE KNITTING WORKSHOP

"Hurry up, Jenny! Let's get inside before the next shower," Carole said a bit forcefully as Jenny grabbed her shoulder bag and stepped out of Carol's Ford Fiesta car. Carol quickly pressed the remote key for the door, slung her own knitting bag over her arm and headed for the library entrance with Jenny close behind. There were only ten minutes to go before the knitting workshop started.

Jenny noticed a motley crew of women, plus a few men, getting out of other cars or walking from a nearby bus stop with an array of plastic bags or baskets in their hands. They seemed to be all ages, shapes and sizes, from teenagers to well-retired folks! Some quietly chatted amongst themselves as they headed towards the library entrance door before being greeted by a friendly doorman as they stepped inside.

"Guess you're the crafty bunch," he said. "Just head to the Lagan Room at the back of the building, but watch the wet paint on the walls near the loos!" Carole and Jenny then followed the crowd to the hall where the workshop was due to start. About twenty other people seemed to have already arrived, and Jenny couldn't help thinking that a lot of them looked more like natters than knitters!

A tall woman with her black hair tied into a bun stood in a corner and held up a beautiful laced sweater that seemed almost complete. "Doesn't her hairstyle look at bit like Miss Kershaw's?" Carole whispered, as Jenny felt a bit of a shiver going down her spine. She really didn't want to meet folks here that reminded her of that awful teacher.

"I must admit it does," Jenny responded, "but I think she looks as lot nicer!" A blond, tousled-haired teenager who looked about fourteen was leaning over a table with small cardboard circles and pieces of wool in her hand, no doubt making bobbles for some project, and seemed to be chatting to the Miss Kershaw look-a-like. "Blimey, I love your sweater. I wish you'd make me one like that," she was saying. "I can't stop getting my wool tangled, and I'm only trying to make some decorations for smoothie bottle tops!"

Another woman at the same table was setting out small squares in rows, no doubt to join into some kind of blanket. She'd pretty, copper-coloured hair cut in a bob, and everything about her looked neat and orderly. Another woman with a lilting Scottish accent who was sitting beside her pulled a beautiful Arran jumper out of a Tesco bag, full of interesting stitches and bobbled edges. Jenny had expected most of the knitters in the class to be retired silver surfers with gold-rimmed glasses and pension books, but lots of the folk in the room looked a lot younger than herself! She was amazed at the range of their projects, everything from colourful sweaters, scarves and hand-crafted toys, to cuddly teddy bears and a knitted replica of a famous local footballer!

However, not everyone seemed to be making something elaborate. A couple of teenagers who looked about sixteen, were each holding up what looked like the beginning of a scarf on big needles.

"Help, I need you to pick up my dropped stitches. I can't get my wool to stay on these needles," one of them pleaded with the other, as she looked despairingly at her work. Jenny couldn't help thinking this reminded her of the scarf she'd attempted in Miss Kershaw's class years before! At the rear of the hall a few men were shifting tables and chairs, whilst a couple of boys who looked about ten and a curly-haired woman set out mugs and plates of biscuits on another table at the side of the room.

Carole gently steered Jenny over to a small round table where a few others had already gathered and had started to open their knitting project bags. Most of their bags seemed pretty full, with at least one pair of knitting needles protruding from the top!

Carole pulled out one of the chairs at this table and spoke to Jenny. "Here's a chair for you. I'll sit over there." Carole walked around to the other side of the group while Jenny sat down and smiled shyly at the rest of the knitters.

One of the group, who looked quite trendy with short cropped hair, skinny jeans and a gold-hooped earring in each ear, turned and spoke to Jenny. "Hi, I'm Kylie. I'm not sure what we're going to learn tonight, but Marie's always got some great ideas up her sleeves! Last winter she showed us how to make a simple tree decoration using different colours of wool and I managed to make one myself. I even got orders for three more!"

"Sounds great," responded Jenny. "Maybe I'll learn something like that too!"

The woman with the glossy copper bob then introduced herself to Jenny. "Hi, I'm Leanne," she said. "Did you have far to come to get here?"

"No, I didn't," Jenny replied. "My friend Carole gave me a lift. It only took about ten minutes in her car."

Leanne seemed happy with that information, before she lifted up one of her small knitted squares from the table and handed it to Jenny. Jenny gently grasped the small piece of knitted cloth in her hand as Leanne continued to chat. "If I ever get this blanket finished, I'm sending it to a school called Hope Academy in Sierra Leone, where my daughter Carley works as a teacher. She emails me each week and regularly asks for donations of knitted blankets and small garments. Some of this class have already sent her items through a shipping company based in Belfast Harbour. One of these days, I'd love to hear a little story about a child at the school receiving one of these gifts. Some of them have been affected by the awful Ebola virus that was on the news this week."

Jenny remembered hearing a report about the deadly virus herself and knew she'd love to hear more about Carley's work sometime.

Leanne then opened her cloth knitting bag before she spoke again. "I'm hoping Marie will show me how to join my knitted squares neatly together and make a pretty scalloped finish for the edge of my blanket." Jenny couldn't help thinking while she talked that she reminded her of Auntie Sue when she was about the same age. Sue had also been fine-featured, and wore her hair in a shoulder-length bob.

Jenny briefly started to tell Leanne about her Auntie Sue and her overseas travels in years gone by, whilst Leanne listened with interest and smiled. "I remember she often carried small garments in her baggage. In fact, I found her old knitting bag in the attic last week!" Before Jenny could say anything more another lady at the table stood up and introduced herself.

"Hi, I'm Sally," she said. "Glad to meet you, Jenny." Sally was the lady with the nice soft Scottish accent and wore a pair of pretty rimmed glasses on the bridge of her nose which didn't look like the sort you'd buy in Specsavers! Jenny couldn't help admiring her beautiful arran sweater, which was almost complete.

Another knitter on Jenny's right side then smiled and spoke. "Hi, I'm Lisa," she said. She was obviously making a beautiful christening shawl with a range of small intricate stitches. "I'm sure you're wondering why I'm making this shawl," she quietly said. "I produced a set of twins three months ago and I've been trying to knit each of them a shawl since I heard they were on the way! At the moment, I seem to spend most of my time filling bottles or changing nappies!"

Jenny found this hard to believe, as Lisa had a fabulous figure and didn't look like a woman who'd recently produced twins!

On the other side of the table, another woman at Carole's right hand introduced herself as Pearl. "You're welcome to join us. We're not a bad bunch and we like to do a bit of chatting as we try to do some knitting!" She'd a warm smiley face and bushy auburn hair, and appeared to be knitting some sort of neck scarf.

Jenny had to admit she was glad she'd come to the workshop. All these folks seemed friendly and displayed a range of knitting talents!

As Jenny reached into her own bag and lifted out her small partly-finished sweater, Pearl leaned forward and spoke.

"Hope you get some creative inspiration at this class," she said. "My husband thinks I knit far too much! I hope your husband won't think the same about you!"

Jenny swallowed then replied. "I'm afraid I don't have a husband anymore. He died about eighteen months ago."

"Oh, I'm so sorry, please forgive me," said a quietly shocked Pearl. "I was looking at your wedding ring and just thought a nice young woman like you would be sure to have a husband."

Carole overheard the conversation and quickly stepped in to save any awkwardness. She briefly whispered to Pearl about what happened to Jenny's husband Steve in the tragic Reaville Tower fire.

Leanne, who couldn't help overhearing, then turned towards Jenny and spoke. "I understand a little of what you're going through, Jenny. My brother was a firefighter, and he also died in the course of his work – he was attending a serious road traffic accident where a lorry went on fire."

Jenny quietly thanked Leanne for sharing this, as Pearl quickly apologised again for any awkwardness she'd unwittingly caused.

A few moments later, Marie, the class tutor, made her way to the front of the hall. Her spikey brown hair was cut in a short-cropped style and she was wearing a loose cotton dress topped by an ornate beaded necklace. She also looked about Jenny's age.

Marie then introduced herself. "Hi! Welcome to all of you, whether you're new or been here before. It's great you've come, especially when everyone seems so busy these days. Lots of you are much better knitters than I am, but I hope I can still offer you some pearls of wisdom from what I've learnt over the years!" Jenny couldn't help thinking Marie looked like a free-spirited sort of person who often travelled to far-flung corners of the globe to pick up crafty ideas.

A few moments later, Marie started the workshop with a short talk about some useful knitting techniques, including how to make buttonholes and the best way to pick up a dropped stitch. Jenny didn't realise knitting was such an art, and thought the last technique was a particularly useful one!

The workshop was a bit like being back in Miss Kershaw's craft class, although Marie looked a lot more fashionable and approachable than Miss Kershaw had been!

Over the next hour, Marie slowly worked her way around the room, gently and graciously offering advice and answering queries. When she eventually reached Carole and Jenny's table, she gave Leanne some useful tips on sewing up her knitted squares and how to make a simple scalloped border for the edge of her blanket. She also showed Pearl an easy way of creating a neck opening on her scarf.

When she reached Jenny, Marie asked her what she was making. Jenny lifted her Auntie Sue's little sweater pattern from her bag and showed her what she'd knitted already, plus the story about her Aunt's overseas charity trips! Marie seemed impressed with the small, pretty red garment which was almost complete. As it contained only basic plain and purl stitches and small sleeves knitted into the bodice, there were hardly any borders to worry about!

Marie added, "This is a lovely little sweater, Jenny. You should be proud of yourself. Some small child would love to wear this. What a lovely tribute to your Aunt. Let me know if you need any more help…"

Just as Marie walked off to give advice to someone else, she suddenly turned and came back to Jenny. She demonstrated a simpler way of casting on stitches using one needle and a thumb! Jenny thought this was most helpful and a much easier method than Miss Kershaw's many years before!

After Marie had worked her way around all the knitters in the room and returned to the front of the hall, she gently raised her voice and asked each person to stop what they were doing. Some had achieved quite a lot: others had spent a lot of time chatting! She then announced, "Supper's ready. Hope you can stay for a quick cuppa and a bit more chat! There's another workshop in two weeks' time and I hope you'll all come back! This will be the last one before the Halloween break."

Just then, the lady with the curly hair who'd been putting out the mugs and biscuits with her young helpers at the start of the evening, appeared with two large flasks, one containing coffee and the other tea. As she walked around the tables pouring hot drinks, Jenny continued to chat to a few of her new-found knitting friends. Waiting for their mugs to be filled, Pearl also offered

Jenny some small motifs which she'd planned to use as decorations on some small cardigans but no longer required.

"I don't think I'll need these now," she said. "You're welcome to them, Jenny," as she then handed over a small plastic bag with seven small motifs inside.

"Many thanks, Pearl." Jenny responded. "You're very kind, but I'd like to pay you for these."

"Not at all," replied Pearl. "Please accept them as a small gift. No doubt you'll do something useful with them."

After supper finished, the knitters and natters spent a short while finishing off what they could of their projects before the workshop stopped for the evening. Jenny managed to sew one of Pearl's motifs, a little flower, onto the front of her small now-completed sweater and felt chuffed with the end result. The little garment had surprisingly turned out like the one in Auntie Sue's pattern! If Miss Kershaw had been around, she'd be in shock to see how Jenny's knitting skills had improved! "Maybe after an early shift next week, I might even start another one!" Jenny couldn't help thinking to herself.

Eventually everyone started to pack up to go home. Pearl had managed to finish her scarf and twin mum Lisa had even completed her shawl! Carole, who'd always been a quick knitter, had made a small woolly hat for one of her nephews as a wee gift to put away as a Christmas stocking filler!

It didn't take long for everyone to gather up their bags and leave the Lagan Room, with promises to meet again in two weeks' time. As they headed along the corridor to the library's front door, Jenny noticed the same friendly doorman on duty, reminding everyone to "mind the wet paint on the corridor walls!" She then followed Carole outside to the car, when she had to admit she'd had an interesting evening. She'd learnt a bit more about knitting, met some nice friendly folks and was inspired to make some more little sweaters...

Just as Carole and Jenny reached the car, another huge shower came on. "Better jump in quickly!" Carole said as she unlocked the front doors and the two ladies quickly got inside, while heavy rain beat against the windows and muddy puddles appeared on the ground. A few moments later, as Carol started the car engine, there was a loud tap at the window. She pressed the remote button to open the window on the passenger side as Jenny came face to face with a rather damp Leanne from their table at the workshop.

Leanne was holding out a small piece of paper as she spoke. "I thought I'd catch up with you two. I wanted to give you this note, Jenny. It's the contact address for my daughter, Carley, in Africa. I know you asked for this during supper. She'd welcome any small items for her school kids."

Jenny thanked Leanne for this information. She was genuinely interested to hear more about the work of this young teacher in Sierra Leone and to try to give her some support.

About ten minutes later, as the rain thankfully eased, Carole pulled up outside Jenny's house. Jenny quickly gathered up her bag and soggy umbrella, then asked Carole, "Would you like to pop in for a few moments?"

Carole replied, "If you don't mind, Jenny, I'll head on. Tracey heads off to Sudan tomorrow and I promised I'd help her finish her packing. I've to give her a lift to the airport at seven o'clock in the morning so I'll need a few hours' sleep myself! By the way, I thought the wee sweater you knitted was lovely. You put a lot of effort into it, and the red colour is nice and bright. I even liked the little motif you sewed on the front!"

Jenny quickly asked Carole another question as she reached into her knitting bag and pulled out the finished sweater. "Carole, I want to ask you a favour. Could you to pass this onto Tracey? She might be able to give it to a small child at the Refugee Camp where she's going to do her placement."

"Jenny, I'd be delighted," said Carole." I know Tracey will love to share her experiences with you when she comes back. No doubt she'll have plenty of stories to tell!"

Jenny then got out of the car and waved to her friend as she walked up the path to her front door, whilst Carole headed off to get Tracey's packing sorted …

CHAPTER FOUR

YAYA'S STORY (SUDAN)

"I don't remember so much dust up here before. I could do with a quick shower!" Jenny muttered to herself a she climbed down the short ladder from the attic. She then gave a slight cough as she grabbed a tissue from a pocket in her jeans and blew her nose to try to stop sneezing. She'd just spent two hours clearing more of Steve's items from the attic, including packing his old books into cardboard boxes for donation to a local second-hand book-shop and squeezing his former firefighter uniforms which his fire station colleagues might still be able to use into a large plastic sack. Jenny had already arranged for volunteers from a local youth club to collect his keep fit items, which had been put into suitcases and were to be passed onto some deprived young people that they knew.

Jenny then headed over into the bathroom to take her quick shower. After slowly undressing, Jenny stepped into the bath and lifted the over-bath showerhead from its hook on the wall. As she turned on the taps and let the warm water cascade over her body, she whispered "This is bliss!" then grabbed the shower gel and gave her body a good scrub, watching the attic dust flow away from her skin. A couple of minutes later, she switched off the water, lifted the shower head back onto it's base and slowly climbed over the side of the bath.

Jenny quickly dried herself with a towel before reaching for her new pair of jeans and sweatshirt, which were lying over the radiator and which she'd bought in Dunnes Stores. She then gave her hair a quick comb before walking to her small rear bedroom which was now a neat office-cum-study. There wasn't a lot of space in this room. Several boxes stacked away in a corner held some of Steve's old bank statements, which now needed to be shredded, and an old bookcase stood along one of the walls. There was also a small sofa beside the window, a mottled beige mat on the floor and a small computer desk that Jenny planned to use for her laptop. She'd only recently got a computer and was still unclear about some of its functions. "I must try and join a wee computer class one of these days and learn a bit more about the IT world," she thought to herself, as she walked over to the computer and switched it on.

As the machine booted up and a range of icons appeared, Jenny clicked twice on the Microsoft Outlook icon and a few moments later some emails appeared on the screen. She spotted three messages from friends, a delivery notice from B&Q about some gardening tools she'd ordered, and an Air Miles advertisement about cheap summer holidays. As she scanned further down the screen, Jenny noticed an email from an unfamiliar address. She felt a bit wary about opening it then suddenly remembered it could be from Tracey, Carole's niece, and it seemed quite long. Jenny clicked open the email and was really touched and challenged by what she read...

Hi Jenny
Sorry I didn't get to thank you for your little red jumper before I left. It fitted into my suitcase and it was put to good use! I passed it onto a little girl who had a nasty hand injury and it really cheered her up.
I can't believe I've been here in Juba for nearly four weeks. It seems no time since I jetted off from London and arrived in Sudan eight hours later. I was really excited to get my first glimpse of Africa through the aircraft window and I couldn't believe the heat when I stepped off the plane. After what seemed like ages in passport control, I was met by Sam, who'd come from the Refugee Camp to collect me in a jeep that had seen better days and had an exhaust that was about to fall off! After four attempts at starting the engine, Sam drove me through the early morning Khartoum traffic and onto Juba in the South West corner of the country.
It took six hours to get here! On the way, I noticed lots of animal skeletons and broken vehicles by the side of the bare clay roads, with big potholes in lots of places! I dread to think what the roads would be like in the rainy season. We also drove through small villages with stray dogs and goats roaming around. The goats looked awfully like sheep!

It wasn't hard to find our Camp in Juba as it's surrounded by a large fence and most days you can spot several jeeps coming or going and maybe a helicopter circling overhead. There's lots of makeshift shelters made from tied bamboo branches and plastic tarpaulin roofs, where lots of young women and children currently live.

Mike is our Senior Doctor and he directed me to a small glorified tent at the back of the Camp which has been my wee den ever since. My bed is a small canvas-covered mattress on the floor with a murky white pillow at one end and a rough woolly blanket on top. I've a white metal basin on the floor beside the bed which I often use as a bath as the makeshift showers aren't working! The food's not bad, although I mainly eat lots of beans and bananas. I've been really busy here, helping with emergencies, or working with Margit, a Dutch nurse in charge of the children's feeding programme. We treat hundreds of small patients each day, often weighing small underweight babies at a large tree with a scale hanging from a branch with a small sling underneath. I frequently measure the circumference of the babies' or small children's arms with a tape that displays different coloured bands. If the fastened tape reaches the red band, the baby or child needs extra feeding with a Plumpy'Nut supplement or fortified porridge to build up their strength. Sadly, some of the wee kids have runny eyes, dry skin, or diarrhoea, and a few have large swollen bellies caused by hunger.

I've also been doing lots of first aid and helped Doctor Mike in the operating theatre with some basic surgery, but nothing too complicated as I haven't done my main surgery training yet. I know lots of people in the Camp have walked hundreds of miles to get here from various parts of the country. I've heard the names Rumbek, Abyei, Bor and Nasir as some the towns they've come from.

Last week, I noticed a little girl who seemed alone in the Surgical Ward. She looked underfed, her right hand was covered with a bandage and she couldn't lift her arm. Every few minutes, she gently coughed through chattering teeth. When I examined her with my stethoscope, I could hear her small rapid heartbeats and shallow breathing. One of the Camp nurses spoke her tribal language and found out her name was Yaya. She'd travelled about 100 kilometres to get here which must have been an awful journey to make. As I searched for a small blanket or garment to place over her body which shivered and shook with a possible fever, I suddenly had an idea...

I remembered your small red jumper that I'd put in the base of my ruck-sack, so quickly raced back to my tent and grabbed it, then ran back to give it to Yaya. It didn't take long to stretch the small jumper over her tiny, frail body whilst her small face broke into a beautiful smile. Soon afterwards, she dropped off to sleep and slept soundly through that night. Next morning, Yaya looked a lot better than the day before. Her shaking fits had stopped, and her pulse had returned to normal. I took the band-age off her hand and noticed the nasty wound underneath had started to heal. Yaya told one of the Camp nurses that someone had stood on her hand, shortly after she'd arrived in the Camp. She'd also damaged three fingers whilst she escaped from her village one night. Yaya's hand now has a good chance of healing if she keeps it rested and gets enough proper food for her body to mend.

A couple of days ago, a quiet but dignified young woman, wearing a few simple beaded necklaces around her neck, walked into Yaya's ward. It was Yaya's mother, and she'd walked to the Camp with Yaya and several others after a rebel attack on their village. Her other child, Yaya's small brother, had got separated during their long walk to the Camp but he's since been found. He's also received food supplements at the children's feeding programme. I watched Yaya's mother gently helping her small daughter to stand up whilst she held onto her stronger hand and assisted her to walk. Yaya was wearing her little red knitted jumper at the time. It looked just the right size for her body and her mother seemed delighted that her daughter had received such a lovely small garment.

Yaya, her mother, and her little brother will soon leave the Camp to return to their village and I know Yaya will take her new red jumper with her. She'll be able to wear it during chilly evenings when temperatures drop, and she might even lend it to another needy child someday...

I've seen lots of small donated garments in the Camp, but your little jumper seemed to be the perfect gift for little Yaya at just the right time. I can't wait to tell you more stories when I get home. I'm off to my Camp bed now...

Warmest greetings.

Tracey

Jenny looked forward to hearing more about little Yaya and Tracey's work at the Camp when she returned to Belfast...

CHAPTER FIVE

ROBERT'S STORY (BELFAST)

Jenny looked down at her nursing rota as she walked out of the Health Centre towards her small black Fiat Panda. "Glad I've a half day!" she muttered to herself as she got ready for another morning's work. "I really hope the Solicitor starts finalising Steve's legal matters today and advises me about paying off his funeral fees."

Jenny planned to finish around lunchtime, as her appointment was at two o'clock. At least she wasn't timetabled for the afternoon Outpatient Clinic, as it wasn't Wednesday or Friday, nor was she on the Saturday daytime or evening rota this week. She'd only District Nursing patients to see, but that could mean anything from checking blood sugars to bandaging toes! Jenny always had to be prepared for an emergency, so kept an additional medical bag in her car boot, filled with a range of useful supplies.

Jenny noticed Robert Smith was the first patient on her morning rota. She'd met him at the Health Centre about a month earlier, when he'd arrived for treatment for a hand and arm injury, and it was an awkward time for him to have had an accident. His young wife, Jodie, had just given birth to twins, Tom and Eloise. Robert lived about two miles from the Health Centre so Jenny slowly drove into the busy Tuesday traffic, giving herself extra time as it was a bitterly cold November morning, and she didn't want her car skidding on roads which were now well covered with fallen leaves! She'd only bought her little Fiat a short time before Steve died, and needed it to last a fair while.

Jenny soon spotted Robert and Jodie's small, neat suburban town house in a fairly quiet, mainly working-class area and was impressed with what she saw. A large horse chestnut tree stood proudly in the front garden, surrounded by a pebble path leading to a red front door with a small tub of winter pansies at each side. As Jenny pulled up at the front gate, she noticed the living room blinds were still drawn, but a light was on in an upstairs bedroom. Jenny walked up the path and rang the doorbell.

Robert answered the door. Jenny hadn't forgotten his tired but happy face when she'd met him before, but she now saw it again as he invited her into the house.

"Jenny, it's great to see you at this time of time of day," Robert said quickly. "Sorry I was in a bit of a state the last time you met me, being a new father of twins isn't an easy job! It's great, the wee guys are thriving, but poor Jodie's exhausted with all the sleepless nights."

"No problem, Robert," Jenny replied. "People like you keep me in a job."

Jenny knew that Robert and Jodie were about the same age as herself, although Robert didn't look it, and if her memory served her right, he normally worked as a long-distance lorry driver. She was also aware that Tom and Eloise had arrived a little early and spent their first two weeks in an incubator. One of Jenny's nursing colleagues, also based at the Health Centre, still called each week to check their progress and give Jodie some useful advice.

Robert led Jenny into a cosy sitting room, where a green leather sofa leaned against one wall and a modern recessed fireplace was set into another. A Mother and Baby magazine plus a couple of tiny Pampers' nappies also lay on top of a small coffee table in the centre of the room. Jenny quickly spotted two small Moses baskets in a corner, as a small cry came out of one of them.

Just then, Jodie came rushing into the room. She looked tired, but also had a rosy glow as she turned to speak to Jenny. "Jenny, I don't know what we'd have done without the support of nurses like you, both for Robert and the twins. I must confess Thomas and Eloise haven't slept much since they came home and your colleague Sharon's been really helpful. She's due back later this week."

Jenny knew Sharon would be a good support. She often bumped into Jenny at the Health Centre staff room, where they'd always plenty to talk about. Sometimes she went off on volunteering trips overseas, a bit like Aunt Sue had done, and Jenny was always interested to hear her stories on her return.

Jenny couldn't help noticing that Robert, who was now standing beside the kitchen door, seemed a bit anxious, and appeared to want to talk.

"Jenny," he said, "I don't think you were aware of this, but I lost my job just before I met you at the Health Centre last month. Jodie and I've been pretty devastated as it was an awful shock to lose a regular wage at this time in our lives, just after the birth of the twins." Robert continued, "Of course you'll know about my lorry accident in France where I was hit by another vehicle just outside Calais port."

Jenny had heard about the accident; Robert was carrying goods from a London department store to Paris when several boxes became dislodged and fell into the driver's cab, crushing several bones in his arm and hand.

"I've not been allowed back to work since, as my boss thought I'd be a liability and has offered my job to someone else. Jodie and I got a bit of a lump sum from the company which is helping us to buy Christmas presents and items for the babies, but it's not going to last us long and we're trying to do everything we can on a budget. I've had to start a wee voluntary job in the meantime." Jenny was concerned for Robert and Jodie having to deal with a shock like this in addition to Robert's injury.

A few moments later, Jenny put on her new reading glasses and took a look at Robert's left upper limb. She noticed it was healing well, but a few angry-looking scars and bruises still covered the skin at the back of his hand and smallest finger. Thankfully, he could now bend his wrist and elbow and move all his fingers, which he couldn't the month before. While Jenny completed her examination, Robert shared more details about his new voluntary part-time lorry driving job for a charity that brought aid to Romania in Eastern Europe. This involved driving from Northern Ireland via a sea crossing to Liverpool in England, then down the length of England to Dover in the South. After crossing the Channel Tunnel, there was further driving on the continent, through France, Belgium and Germany, then into Romania. Another driver called Chris, whom Robert had done some charity work with in the past, planned to join him on his next trip.

"We carry all sorts of goods on each journey," Robert continued, "mostly gifts for orphanage kids or for elderly persons in rural villages. In Transylvania district there's lots of needy folks from Roma families. On this next trip I plan to deliver Christmas shoeboxes filled with children' gifts, tins of corned beef, packets of dried pasta, cooking oil, washing powder, nappies, blankets, kitchen utensils and toiletries. I also hope to carry several crates of clothes, including warm woollen hats, scarves, gloves, and some small knitted jumpers. A number of the jumpers will be given to children from poverty-stricken families or to others who live in a huge orphanage until they're sixteen, when they could be forced to leave. Many can end up on the streets." Jenny was horrified to hear these facts, but glad that drivers like Robert and Chris were willing to give their time and skills to help these people.

"When do you next leave, Robert?" Jenny then asked.

He replied, "I'm heading off on Monday. Jodie's mother is coming to stay whilst I'm away, but Chris and I shouldn't be gone for more than a week."

Jenny had a sudden thought then posed another question, "Robert, would you be able to make use of a small tunic-style sweater for a child of about three or four years? I mean, to take it with you to Romania?"

Robert replied, "I certainly wouldn't say no to an offer like that!"

Jenny smiled faintly as she continued, "I've recently done a bit of knitting myself and have just finished a small garment for a child that size. In fact, I've actually put it in my work bag." Jenny then walked across the room towards her bag. She'd managed to knit this small sweater from Auntie Sue's pattern over the previous few evenings and had also sewn a small train motif onto the front.

At that moment, Jodie walked into the room and headed over to the small Moses baskets where she gently lifted up Eloise, who'd now started to whimper slightly. "I'd better feed this little lady,"

Jodie said, as she rocked Eloise in her arms. "She can be a little slow. Tom's already had his fill, he should be settled for a while." Jenny noted little Eloise had a lot of her mother's features.

As Jodie took Eloise out of the room, Jenny lifted the small sweater from her bag and gave it to Robert.

"That's kind of you, Jenny," said Robert. "I'll get Jodie to put this into one of the boxes we're preparing for the lorry. She's been sorting loads of bags and boxes for this trip and is a lot more organised than I am! When I get back, I'll let you know how things went, and might be able to tell you about the child who gets your sweater."

"I'll really appreciate that, Robert," said Jenny. "Please travel safely with Chris, and I'll look forward to hearing your news. I also wish you every success with any further job interviews!"

Jenny then took another quick look at the injuries on Robert's arm and hand. Apart from a small support bandage over his wrist, the limb seemed strong enough for Robert to drive. She agreed she'd review it again on Robert's return from Romania.

Jenny then glanced at her watch. Nearly half an hour had passed since she'd arrived, and she'd need to speed up with her other home visits.

After leaving Robert and Jodie's home, the rest of the morning passed quickly. Jenny visited a young Polish woman who'd recently arrived in the country and had a nasty wound on her leg. Her younger sister, who acted as interpreter, told Jenny she'd been bitten by a large dog. As Jenny treated and bandaged the wound, she learned the dog belonged to a neighbour in the same street. She just hoped she didn't meet this dog when she called back to check her patient's wound near the end of the week! Jenny also visited a young businesswoman who'd badly sprained her ankle after falling from a kerb while wearing her high-heeled shoes, a lady in her sixties who'd had a recent stroke and a ninety-year-old retired geography teacher who needed a quick blood pressure check.

At the end of each visit Jenny wrote out a few case notes which she planned to copy onto a computer when she got back to the Health Centre.

In what seemed like no time, it was 1.30pm. Jenny completed her notes, managed a quick lunch, then left work to head into town.

After parking her car near the new Waterfront Concert Hall, Jenny arrived at the Solicitor's Office to finalise the remaining parts of Steve's legal estate. Miss Jones, a Company Legal Secretary, greeted Jenny as she walked into the office building. "Please take a seat, Mrs O'Neill," she said, "Mr Warburton will be free shortly. He's currently dealing with a telephone enquiry." Miss Jones seemed pleasant, with a friendly smile, and wore a pretty turquoise necklace around her neck that matched her short-sleeved cardigan. Jenny sat down and began to thumb through a few magazines on a small table in front as Miss Jones appeared to sort through a pile of legal documents beside a photocopier.

About five minutes later, Miss Jones addressed Jenny again. "Mr Warburton is now free. Please make your way to his office on the first floor, which you'll find at the second door on the right as you reach the top of the staircase." Jenny thanked Miss Jones for her help then made her way to the first-floor office, where she was met at the door by Mr Warburton himself.

"Good afternoon, Mrs O'Neill, please come in and sit down," he uttered as he waved Jenny towards a seat near his desk. "It's my privilege to be at your assistance." Mr Warburton was a smart, fresh-faced man of forty, who seemed friendly and efficient and had briefly met Steve about six months before he died, when he'd gone to watch the local Fire and Rescue Service playing a friendly football match. "Steve was a really nice guy," Mr Warburton said. "So sad a young chap like him to have to leave us so soon in such a terrible tragedy, especially when he was trying to save other lives. I remember he told me at that match that he really enjoyed his work. He also spoke well of you! Please don't hesitate to contact me anytime Mrs O'Neill, if I can be of help to you."

Mr Warburton began to sift through the large pile of documents in front of him, explaining their contents to Jenny, and helping her to sign off necessary papers, before reminding her to phone again if she needed to make another appointment.

When Jenny eventually left Mr Warburton's office, about an hour later, she decided to do a quick bit of shopping while she was still in the city centre, including looking for a winter coat. As she passed the rear entrance of Littlewoods store, she realised she was walking past the small craft shop where she'd bought the wool for the small sweaters she'd already made from Auntie Sue's pattern. In the window was a large sale notice advertising everything at half price.

Jenny decided to enter the shop and noticed the basket beside the door was still half-filled with balls of wool, the same type she'd used for Yaya's and the other small sweater.

As there were only ten left and the whole batch cost £20 at sale price Jenny decided to buy the lot. "I might as well fork out a wee bit of money," she thought. "Maybe I'll get time to knit a few more sweaters!" As she walked up to the counter to ask if she could purchase the wool in the basket Jenny recognised the sales assistant she'd seen before.

"You're back again! Hope the knitting's going okay!" the assistant said in recognition. "I guess you're looking for those other red balls of wool at the door." Jenny smiled and nodded as the assistant walked over to the basket and carried it to the counter. "I'll give you these as a wee bargain and you can have another 10% off. Maybe you'll come back another time and buy more wool from the shop," she quickly added as she packed the wool into two paper bags.

Jenny responded, "No doubt I will," as she lifted a purse from her bag to pay for the goods.

"By the way, I'm Jean," mentioned the sales assistant. "Hope to see you soon again."

Jenny then replied, "Thanks very much and I look forward to making some more little garments from your wool."

On leaving the shop a few moments later, Jenny walked towards Marks and Spencer to have a look at the range of winter coats. This was a good move as the weather was definitely getting chillier and she couldn't help thinking that Robert and Chris were going to be even colder as they travelled to Romania the following week with their lorry full of charity goods. Jenny hoped her small donated sweater would reach some small child who badly needed a woolly tunic at this wintry time of year.

CHAPTER SIX

OFF TO ROMANIA

"Hey Chris," said Robert, "I'm glad this is the last checkpoint, my back's killing me after all these miles of driving. I hope Border Customs don't keep us waiting here as long as the French and German ones did."

"I hope so, too." Chris responded. "They're a bit scary looking and I'm not sure they'll understand us when we try to tell them what's in the back of the lorry. Guess we'd better get our passports ready."

A few moments later one of the Romanian Border Guards stepped forward and motioned for them to stop. Robert put the lorry into first gear, pressed his foot onto the brake then brought the vehicle to a standstill as the Guard gazed down at the registration number, recording it in a small black book.

After this the Guard turned around, looked up at the cab and abruptly announced, "Passports please." Robert and Chris reached into the rucksacks behind their seats and pulled out their respective passports, which they then handed through the window to the Guard. Robert also offered him a small envelope for inspection which contained some charity documentation authorising items to be transported from the United Kingdom. The guard reached up, grasped the forms and quickly scanned the contents. He was obviously able to understand the English writing. A few moments later, he said, "Please depart your vehicle and unlock the rear doors." Robert pressed the control switch to release the rear doors then stepped out of the cab as Chris climbed out the other side.

The Guard then gave a small gasp and looked surprised as the rear doors slowly opened. He couldn't believe the huge number of filled shoe boxes and other donated goods inside. He quickly uttered, "Go to Office and wait," as he obviously wanted to complete a search. Chris and Robert headed over to the "Office", which was basically a small room with an old burning gas stove, broken windows, two wooden chairs and various certificates on the walls. A few mugs also sat on top of a desk that was covered with a range of files and paper documents. Robert lifted a copy of a local Romanian newspaper that was lying on a nearby chair, but he obviously couldn't translate any of the headlines. Chris couldn't either.

"I hope we're not kept here too long," Robert muttered, "I'd really love to touch base with the orphanage before dark."

"I agree," Chris responded, "my toes feel numb after sitting so long and I'm looking forward to some sleep – haven't had forty winks since we left Belfast. I think the temperature's dropped since we crossed the last Border, too."

Robert and Chris kept chatting until they began to feel quite drowsy then Robert checked his watch and noticed another hour had gone by. At that point he looked outside and suddenly uttered, "Looks like we're getting the go ahead," as the Guard was now closing the rear door of the lorry and heading back to the office.

The Guard entered the room, handed Robert the two passports that belonged to himself and Chris plus the charity paper documentation and said, "I have finished checking your vehicle and paperwork. Please return to your transport and drive towards the exit sign. Welcome to our country."

Without further ado, Robert and Chris returned to the lorry, settled into their seats and prepared to move on.

Shortly after leaving the Border crossing, Robert and Chris drove on through several small villages framed by the Transylvanian mountains in the distance, and headed for the town of Dej, not far from Oradea, the capital city. As they reached the outskirts of Dej, they noticed a range of cars, bicycles and horse-drawn carriages on the roads. The carriage drivers appeared to be farmers transporting hay and other goods from a local market.

A few minutes later they spotted a large grey stone building up ahead as Robert said, "Hey Chris, I think this is the orphanage we're looking for. It looks like the one in the photo from Head Office." Chris agreed. "You're right, Robert. I think we've reached the end of our journey." It seemed identical to the one that some of their charity colleagues had visited the year before.

As Robert slowly steered the lorry off the main road to Oradea and onto a shorter pothole-filled road that led to the large stone orphanage building, it didn't take long to find the entrance. He carefully negotiated the gate then drove up the main path, covered by a few broken flagstones and weeds, and brought the lorry to a standstill outside the front door.

Robert and Chris slowly staggered out of the lorry and walked towards the short flight of cracked steps that led to the heavy wooden door with a large rope hanging alongside to activate a bell.

Robert slowly tugged the rope three times, resulting in three clanging chimes from the bell. A few moments later there was the sound of footsteps and someone answered the door. A stern looking woman, aged about fifty, pushed down on the large wooden latch and the door slowly opened, giving out a loud creaking sound as it moved.

The lady spoke slightly hesitant English with a high-pitched voice. "Hello, I expect you. My name is Druscilla and I'm Director of this Institution. I recognise your lorry from last year. Your organisation make children happy. I know you make us happy again."

Robert and Chris immediately knew she was the person they'd been instructed to report to, as they'd already seen a photograph of her in Belfast. As Druscilla demonstrated a fair command of the English language, she continued in a brusque voice, "Please drive lorry to parking area at the rear of building, then come back here and I take you to my office." Chris stood at the doorway with Druscilla before she said anything else as Robert lifted the lorry's keys from his pocket and headed back to the vehicle to drive it to the rear of the building. Chris waited for his return.

A few minutes later, as Robert walked back towards the main entrance, he couldn't help feeling a sharp wind chill and a bleakness in the place. He could see that a number of windows were cracked, and pale sickly-green coloured paint was peeling off several inside and outside walls. Several doors also seemed to be held up by broken hinges. Both Robert and Chris already knew it was a difficult environment for the children who lived there, but they certainly hadn't realized it was such a large place.

As Robert re-entered the building to join Druscilla and Chris, he could hear jumbled voices and screams coming from a number of children who walked shyly into a large hallway, some looking as young as two years old. They were all wearing faded torn trousers and T shirts, plus a stained sweater or cardigan with several holes, and far too big for their thin, fragile bodies. Some of them shivered in the cold with runny noses, and they all looked as if they could do with a good square meal.

As Robert joined Druscilla and Chris in the hallway, Druscilla gave a sharp command, "You come to my Office. Follow me. I give you more instructions." Robert and Chris quickly followed her to her first-floor office, reached via a long winding staircase at the end of a corridor. Robert and Chris were surprised when they reached this room, as it appeared to be of a much higher standard than the rest of the building. On one side stood a huge cloth-covered sofa, whilst in the middle of the floor was a sturdy wooden table, surrounded by four metal-framed chairs. Several pictures hung on the walls, mainly winter scenes of small villages which Robert faintly recognised as having passed through on the drive to Dej. The sturdy wooden table turned out to be Druscilla's main desk.

Druscilla then turned towards Robert and Chris and gave a further command, "Please sit down and be comfortable," as she motioned for them to each sit on one of the metal-framed chairs. She then walked across the room and opened a narrow wooden door on the wall opposite her desk, displaying a tiny walk-in cupboard inside, with a small sink and boiler plus a neat worktop. Druscilla lifted a tray from the worktop containing three ceramic cups, a plate of biscuits and a silver coloured teapot, and carried this over to her desk. After pouring hot tea into each of the cups, she then handed one to Robert and another to Chris before offering them a biscuit from the plate.

Both guys uttered a quiet "Thank you," to Druscilla as they hadn't eaten or drunk for hours and were thankful for these snacks, even though they each thought the tea had quite a strange flavour and tasted as if it had been boiled with milk and sugar, which it had.

A few minutes later, when Robert had finished his tea, he asked Druscilla, "Could I make a quick comfort stop?" Druscilla knew what this meant and gave him some directions to a downstairs toilet. Robert stood up, walked past Chris, and left the Office to go downstairs, walking back along the same corridor and winding staircase as before. Leading off from this corridor, Robert couldn't help noticing several rooms which looked like sparsely decorated old hospital wards, lined with rows and rows of metal cots and beds. Several small children lay on top of the cots and beds, staring blankly at the ceiling while others were seated on the floor, rocking from side to side, or bumping their head against one of the walls. This was most disturbing to see.

After descending the winding staircase, Robert soon found the toilet, a tiny room with a wooden door at the end of another short corridor. The toilet itself was basically a small latrine that looked more like a hole on the ground. A roll of damp toilet paper lay on the floor, with a broken piece of soap balanced near a wobbly tap at the sink. A small blue bucket also hung underneath a leaking tap on the wall. This appeared to be the main flush for the toilet.

Robert made use of the toilet as quickly as he could before returning to Druscilla's office on the first floor. As he re-entered her room, Druscilla spoke again. "I have talk with Chris about unloading items from the lorry." She then started to clarify plans about a children's party to be held the following day in the main hall of the building and mentioned the filled shoe boxes and most of the other donated goods on the lorry would to be given out to the orphanage children at the end of the party. A few other kids from local poverty-stricken families were also invited to attend.

Druscilla then confirmed, "I have arrangements made for you both to stay at a small local hostel, and you may go there after unpacking lorry." Robert and Chris quickly agreed to return to the lorry and to start unloading the contents before it got any darker. Druscilla seemed pleased and waved them off as she quietly added, "I see you at party tomorrow."

As Robert and Chris walked back outside, they noticed the light was already starting to fade and knew they needed to complete the lorry unloading as quickly as possible. With limited lighting around the building, it also took a lot longer than expected to unpack the goods. In fact, it was a good hour's work to lift out the shoeboxes and other items and to stack them in the main hall where Druscilla indicated the planned party was to take place. While Robert and Chris worked, a few orphanage staff members came out to meet them and offered to help, but Druscilla appeared and told them to go back to their duties. Several orphanage children also watched from an upstairs window whilst cries and shouts could be heard from a downstairs room.

Robert and Chris felt sorry for the children as they seemed to have so little. They couldn't wait to see happiness on their faces when they received their gifts the next day...

Eventually the lorry was emptied. All the shoe boxes and other gifts had been stacked in the hall and Robert and Chris were now ready to leave. Robert pressed the control switch to close the rear doors of the vehicle and climbed into the cab whilst Chris read out written instructions for finding the Hostel. He'd managed to get these from Druscilla as he'd waited for Robert in her office. Chris then jumped back into the lorry himself and said, "I think we're only a few minutes' drive from the Hostel. I'll call out the directions as you do the driving." Robert yawned as he replied, "Great! I guess you're as exhausted as I am, and I can't wait to see my bed for the night! Go ahead and tell me where we're heading!"

Robert started the engine and slowly drove away from the orphanage, as Chris did his best to read out the directions in the limited light, despite a small half-moon shining through the clouds. About five minutes later, the Hostel came into view. Robert parked the now-emptied lorry in a small street, before he and Chris lifted their rucksacks from the back of the cab and stepped outside. They noticed a few beggars further up the street so held onto their bags and made a quick beeline for the entrance of the Hostel.

At the Reception desk check-in, manned by a young lady with dark hair tied into a colourful scarf, Robert and Chris were issued with a key attached to a large wooden keyring and told to proceed to an upstairs room. The Receptionist tried to explain that there was a hot meal ready for them in the dining room on the ground floor; she said, "You get meal when you are ready. It is cooked for you. See room on floor below."

Robert and Chris nodded their thanks then headed upstairs to leave their rucksacks in the bedroom. "I think this is it," said Chris as they reached a green door with a number "8" on the front. "It seems to match the number on the key ring." Robert agreed as they placed the key in the lock, heard a loud squeaking noise as it turned, then slowly opened the door. Two small single beds stood in the middle of the room with a sink in one corner and a large wooden wardrobe at the other. A small window covered with metal bars looked onto the street outside.

After throwing their rucksacks onto their beds, Chris said, "Come on, Robert. Let's leave this stuff and go downstairs. I'm famished!" Robert quickly nodded in agreement, as he felt hungry too. Chris re-locked the bedroom door with the key then they headed back downstairs to the ground floor.

Chris and Robert soon found the dining room in the basement, where they were greeted at the door by a waiter who spoke very fluent English. He had a short, stocky build with grey locks of hair around his face, a short grey beard and not too much hair on the top of his head. He directed Chris and Robert to a small table at the side of the room where their meal was ready. The menu turned out to be beetroot soup, followed by sliced beef on top of black bread. Robert and Chris hungrily tucked into the food, although they found some of the beef a little hard to chew and the bread seemed a bit tough. Whilst they ate, the faces of some of the orphanage kids came into their minds, making them feel quite sad. Those kids certainly weren't going to get a meal like this. Robert also thought about little Tom and Eloise at home. He really wanted to phone Jodie to see if they were okay, but there was no signal or wi-fi to make a connection. He'd just have to wait until his return journey the day after next.

After finishing their evening meal and returning to their room for the night, Robert and Chris prepared for bed then found it hard to get to sleep. The Hostel beds with metal springs in the centre and lumpy mattresses on top weren't the most comfortable, and quite a lot of noise came in from the street outside, including hooting car horns, barking dogs and loud music from another building nearby. Despite exhaustion from driving for miles and unpacking the lorry, their minds also buzzed with some of the orphanage sights and sounds.

Eventually they nodded off.

CHAPTER SEVEN

STEFAN'S STORY (ROMANIA)

Robert grabbed the ringing alarm clock on the top of his rucksack and switched it off. "Oh no, I can't believe it's 5.45am already," he muttered in a sleepy voice as he threw the blanket off the top of his bed and swung his legs onto the floor. It was an early but necessary start, since they needed to get back to the Orphanage by 7.30am. After a good stretch Robert stood up and took a couple of steps over to Chris, who was still in a very deep sleep. He then gave Chris a quick poke in the back before heading over to the small sink at the corner of the room to have a quick wash and shave, as Chris slowly started to stir.

"What's the time?" Chris mumbled in a slurred voice as he lifted his head off his pillow and began to sit up.

"Time to get yourself ready." Robert replied. "We haven't got long to grab some breakfast and head back to the Orphanage. No doubt there will be plenty of jobs for us to do before the afternoon party. If you don't mind, I'll go ahead and get washed." Robert reached towards the sink and switched on one of the taps. An inky grey liquid slowly trickled out for a few seconds, then seemed to stop. "It looks like getting washed is going to be a bit of a challenge! I've just enough water to wet my facecloth. Better see what I can do with it!"

Robert managed to wipe over his face, arms and the front of his trunk but thought he'd better leave the rest of the body until later. Maybe there'd be more water in the evening! He then slowly crossed over the room to put on his clothes which he'd left on the floor beside the bed, as Chris stood up and started to walk over to the sink to get himself washed.

"Hey, Chum," Chris uttered as he glanced at Robert, "I think you've used up all the water. I'll have to give my face a quick clean with one of those small wipes in my luggage and forget about the rest of me! I don't think there's much other choice at the moment!"

Robert and Chris started to chuckle. This water problem was a bit of an adventure, but it also made them aware that many people in Romania had to cope with a challenge like this every day.

A few minutes later, after getting dressed and completing a quick, dry shave, Robert and Chris gathered up their items for the day and left them behind the bedroom door before heading downstairs to the small dining room for breakfast in the Hostel basement. As they arrived, three other guests were already seated at a large table which had been laid out for their meal.

As Robert and Chris sat down, one of the other guests introduced herself as Gina, and explained why she was staying at the Hostel. "I come from Oradea, where I work as a social worker, and I'm here to visit some children at a local orphanage who have come from broken family or have a disability. A number are known to Government Agency or local charity." As Gina spoke, Robert and Chris noted she'd a fair command of the English language, but looked a lot younger and less severe than Druscilla! Her dark blonde hair was tied in a short ponytail at the back of her head and she was wearing a loose flowing skirt which matched the scarf around her neck. Gina continued. "I know the background of every child at the orphanage, and several from nearby villages, including the ones who need special support."

As Robert and Chris then told her briefly who they were and how they were also staying in Dej to deliver charity goods to the same orphanage, a friendly middle-aged couple appeared and set a small plate in front of each guest, topped with a slice of ham, a boiled egg and a wedge of blue cheese. They also brought out a large tray that contained two loaves of sliced bread and a pot of hot tea. Robert and Chris briefly said hello to the other two guests at the table, who were both male and obviously not keen to make conversation, so they started to butter a slice of bread each and pour out their tea. They were both hungry and knew they didn't have much time to spare, so they quickly tucked into their meal whilst they continued to chat to Gina. It turned out Gina was also planning to visit the Orphanage for the afternoon children's party.

"Maybe see you later," she said with a smile as Robert and Chris left the table to return to their bedroom and prepare to leave the Hostel.

It only took a few minutes to attempt cleaning their teeth with some leftover water from a plastic bottle they'd had the day before, complete a quick loo stop and put a couple of extra items into their rucksacks for later in the day, before they headed back downstairs and outside to their lorry parked nearby.

Robert spoke as they walked. "I think we should head along the same road as last night, Chris. I need to take my time with those potholes and there won't be much light at this time of the morning with all those shadows from the overhead trees, but we'll get to the orphanage if we go easy." Chris had to agree as he jumped into the cab behind Robert and threw his rucksack onto the floor at his feet. As Robert then started up the engine and began to drive away from the Hostel, the emerging light of dawn began to appear. Thankfully, it didn't take as long as expected to get back to the Orphanage, despite having to cross several potholes and a few large puddles after a heavy rain overnight.

About fifteen minutes later the Orphanage drive came into view. Robert slowly negotiated his lorry along the long driveway which was poorly lit before bringing the vehicle to a standstill at the rear of the Orphanage building.

Chris lifted both Robert's rucksack and his own from the cab whilst Robert locked the lorry doors, then they both headed towards the Orphanage building. As they entered through the main door on the ground floor, Robert and Chris glanced across the hallway and noticed that several orphanage staff had already set out long wooden tables in the large room where the afternoon Christmas party was to take place. Small plastic plates and beakers, some with several cracks, had been placed at intervals along each table as simple place settings for children. Robert also spotted several large bean bags in a corner, obviously for some of the disabled kids who wouldn't have the postural control to sit at a table.

As Robert and Chris wanted to be helpful, they approached a few of the staff who could speak some English to see if they needed any help but were told that a lot of the party preparations had already been done, although some individual presents still needed to be wrapped for the children. Robert and Chris remembered they'd already unloaded the filled shoeboxes from the lorry the evening before and had transferred extra donated clothes and goods from large bags into small cardboard boxes, also brought indoors from the previous night.

Robert looked at Chris as he then spoke. "I think I'll label each filled cardboard shoebox with the recommended child's age for the goodies inside whilst you can check through the items to see that none are damaged or missing." Chris thought that sounded a good plan and headed with Robert towards the main hall where they'd deposited the lorry's items the evening before. When they reached the hall, they checked to see that all the shoeboxes and bags were still where they'd been left and were glad to note no items were missing. It didn't take long for the two guys to get back to work! By the time each shoebox was checked and labelled, and the other goods wrapped into small paper bags, the morning had sped by!

As lunchtime arrived, Chris turned to Robert and muttered, "I don't know about you, but I'm famished. That was hard work, but I enjoyed it! I'm looking forward to the party!" Just then, one of the staff from the orphanage kitchen, who had quite a wide belly and their hair wrapped up in a scarf, entered the main hall, pushing a large trolley topped by an enormous pan of cabbage soup and a tray of sliced rye bread. Robert and Chris queued up with several of the other orphanage staff to receive a portion of this lunch whilst they attempted to share a few greetings. This resulted in several smiles and giggles as few of the Romanian staff could understand English, and neither Robert nor Chris had a decent grasp of theirs! However, it didn't take long for everyone to get served and to eat their snack meal. Chris mentioned the soup tasted "a bit salty," but Robert thought the rye bread "was quite nice!" and continued, "At least it's not as hard as the Hostel bread this morning!"

In no time, it was afternoon.

The party was ready to start. The main hall had been truly transformed. Large posters of Disney characters hung on the walls, balloons lay in small clumps on the floor and streamers fluttered from the roof. Paper stars were also attached to the curtains at one end of the room, and tiny bunches of plastic flowers were fixed to the end of each table.

A few minutes later, the hall began to fill. Several children who spanned a range of ages rushed into the hall followed by a number of small children in rusty looking wheelchairs, pushed along by some others. Chris noticed some of the kids had walking sticks or metal callipers on their legs as they slowly made their way into the room. All the children seemed to be happy. Some of them were quietly talking amongst themselves, whilst several of the disabled kids who couldn't speak displayed their pleasure by clapping their hands or rocking their heads from side to side.

As the party got underway, a few volunteers from the local village started to organise party games, whilst several orphanage staff escorted children to and from their dormitory rooms. About an hour later, after several party games, including a balloon chase and musical chairs, a party tea was served. Each child was encouraged to sit down at one of the tables in the room, where a few spaces had been left for wheelchair kids. A number of the very frail children were gently placed onto bean bags at one side of the hall; they were also given the chance to enjoy some party food.

As several of the orphanage staff and volunteers served out the goodies, each child at a table received a slice of dry bread, a biscuit, a few potato crisps and a small piece of salami sausage. The more dependent children were served some mashed food by an individual helper.

A short while later, after Robert and Chris had been quietly sitting and talking at the side of the hall, they spotted Gina, the social worker they'd met at the Hostel that morning, appearing through one of the doors. She quickly recognised Robert and Chris from the hostel and came over to chat.

"Hi, Gina," Chris said, "Good to see you. This has certainly been a special afternoon. I didn't realise so many kids lived here, and it's great to see them having fun."

Robert then spoke, "I think they're also enjoying their party meal. I'm sure most of them haven't had a special treat for quite some time."

Gina nodded, "You're right. The best part of the day is still to come. In a few minutes the children will receive a Christmas gift from Santa."

No sooner had she said that than a tall Santa figure emerged through a main doorway from the reception area, pulling a small cart behind him which was filled with a number of shoeboxes and gifts wrapped in Christmas paper. Robert and Chris knew these were mainly items that they'd brought on their lorry from Northern Ireland.

As they watched, several staff members and volunteers then lined up each child to receive a Christmas gift from Santa, including carrying some of the disabled children who were also in the queue. Robert and Chris were really moved to see each child receiving a gift, whether a wrapped shoebox or a present in one of the other wrapped parcels.

Gina turned to Robert and Chris and pointed out some of the non-resident children from the local village, including a little boy who was walking away from Santa, clutching a filled shoebox and a small red sweater. Robert instantly recognised the small garment as the one knitted by Jenny, the district nurse who'd treated his injured hand back at home. A few minutes later, this small boy left the party, as a young woman arrived to accompany him and a few of the other non-orphanage children back to their homes. As they walked out of the hall, Gina shared some information about this little boy and his family. Robert and Chris were touched by the details and hoped his Christmas gifts would be a real blessing. Later on that evening, when they returned to the Hostel and met up with Gina again, they heard how much of a blessing they really were.

Robert knew Chris and himself would never forget this day or place and planned to share the story of the small boy with Jenny, his district nurse, when he got home.

STEFAN

Stefan lived on the outskirts of Dej with his mother Elena and older brother Nicolae, in a part of town where lots of Roma people lived. Their family home was a small shack-like dwelling with no proper windows, a front door held up by rusty hinges and a small kitchen plus two other rooms, with several damp puddles on the floors. Elena and the boys often shivered in the cold, especially in the winter, when outside temperatures could reach -30°. Elena's husband, Andrei, worked in Siberia for most of the year, where he helped to unload cargo for a large shipping company in Vladivostok or sometimes got employment on large submarines that came into the harbour to refuel before they journeyed on the Barents Sea. He only earned a modest wage, but he sent what he could back to his family.

Elena herself found it hard to get work. Like a lot of Roma girls, she had only gone to school for two years and had to leave when she was twelve years old. She could just about read simple words in newspapers or magazines and really wanted to learn to read real books, but had no time or money to buy them. Life with two small boys was hard enough, especially when one had cerebral palsy.

Six-year-old Nicolae had already started school, but Stefan, her younger son, stayed at home. Stefan couldn't walk. Sometimes he tried to stand up and hold onto the small table whilst Elena prepared their meals in their tiny kitchen, but he soon fell down.

His legs couldn't easily support his weight, and his hands often shook when he tried to reach for objects.

Although Elena and Andrei had little money, they were very proud of their two little boys. Elena herself had been brought up in a large orphanage in Oradea, after being abandoned at the age of five by her parents, and never wanted to put her sons into such a place. She could never forget sleeping in a large dormitory with lots of other children in rows of rusted metal beds, including several with disabilities like Stefan. Many of these children never left, and Elena wanted a better life for both her boys.

Every Christmas, Elena tried to purchase a small Christmas gift for her children. She'd already hidden a small wooden train for Nicolae which Andrei had bought in Vladivostok but there was no money left to buy a gift for Stefan. Andrei's small wage only covered enough for one child. Elena couldn't even think of getting Stefan new clothes. There was simply no cash to stretch that far. If only there was some way that she could get him a little gift. Then she remembered Nicolae had been invited to the Christmas party at the local Orphanage with some of the other village children...

"Nicolae, put on your jacket. It's really cold, and there's lots of frost on the ground. Try to keep your shirt clean, I washed it especially for you and it's taken several nights to dry it over the fire. Have a great time at the party and tell us all about it when you come home."

Nicholae slipped the small jacket over his shirt as his Mum gave him a quick hug before he headed for the door. It had been donated by a neighbour called Krisztine, whose own son had outgrown it.

A few moments later, a small cart pulled by a donkey drew up outside. Nicholae jumped onto the cart, owned by one of farmers from outside the village, and waved to his Mum and Stefan as he shouted, "See you later!" before squeezing beside a few of his school friends who were already sitting on the cart.

As Nicholae and the others headed away, poor little Stefan had felt sad. He'd have loved to have gone to the party as well, but couldn't walk there, nor did he have a wheelchair to transport him. He also didn't have a coat or warm jumper to wear. He just had to spend the afternoon sitting in the corner with a small blanket over his legs.

A few hours later, Nicolae returned from the party, in great form. All the children from his school class had received a shoebox filled with treats, including himself. "Hey Mum and Stefan, look what I've got," he uttered as he opened the lid of his shoebox and showed off the goodies inside. He couldn't wait to show them to Elena and Stefan. There were several gifts in the box, including a yellow tennis ball, some chewy sweets, a packet of colouring pencils and a small cloth teddy bear. He also pulled a small brown bag from under his jacket and gave it to Stefan.

"Santa told me you could have this," Nicholae said as he handed it over to his brother.

Stefan's small hands shook as he opened the bag. When he looked inside, he could hardly believe his eyes. "I've got a present just for me!" he then exclaimed as he pulled out a lovely red sweater, knitted in warm double knitting wool.

Nicolae waited for his brother to try on the sweater. "That's cool," he said, as Elena pulled the small garment over Stefan's head. "Now Mum won't have to buy you a new top. It's the same colour as Santa's coat!" Nicolae knew he really needed a new jumper himself, especially for going to school, but was pleased this this one was for Stefan, who needed one even more than himself. Now Stefan could keep warm in the cold winter nights.

"Let me look outside!" Stefan cried as Nicolae gently carried him over to the window overlooking the street outside. Stefan smiled proudly as he looked through the cracked glass panes. He wanted everyone passing by to see him wearing his new sweater. Above all, he was happy that his Mum didn't need to worry about getting enough money to buy him a new sweater herself.

Nicolae then told Stefan, "A big lorry came from Ireland and brought our shoeboxes and lots of other parcels. Even your bright red sweater!" Stefan agreed this was great and he thought it was one of the nicest gifts of all. That night he planned to say a special thank you prayer to God for his lovely new sweater. He knew someone must have knitted it for a young boy like himself...

CHAPTER EIGHT

SHOPPING AT IKEA

Like several other folks, Jenny decided to do some post-Christmas shopping and headed for the large Ikea store at Belfast Harbour Estate. "I can't wait to spend my Christmas vouchers and maybe grab a bargain!" Jenny thought as she pulled into the only parking space she could find.

As she switched off the ignition, reached over the passenger seat to grab her handbag and pulled out a tissue before giving her nose a quick blow, Jenny wiped a few tears from her cheek. She'd had a slight cold over the past few days, but that wasn't the cause of the tears now. She just couldn't help thinking of Steve. Last Christmas had been especially hard without him around, but this year was still a struggle. She also knew she was feeling quite tired. The week before Christmas she'd been especially busy with lots of new patients on her caseload as most of them had been discharged home from hospital for Christmas. At least she'd a few days off now!

After a few minutes, Jenny got out of the car to brave the crowds in Ikea. As she walked across the car park to the entrance of the store, she let her mind drift over some events from the past week. On Christmas Eve, she'd spotted Robert and Jodie Smith walking out of the Spar Garage across the road from the Health Centre, and Robert had rushed over to tell her some great news! He'd been offered a full-time job with the charity that sent him to Romania as a volunteer driver and wanted Jenny to hear about little Stefan and his older brother, Nicolai.

He spoke with a bit of emotion. "Jenny, I knew you'd want to hear where your little red sweater went. A local village child called Nicolae couldn't wait to leave the orphanage party early to bring your little sweater home to his younger brother, whom

I was told had cerebral palsy. I believe his parents weren't able to afford much in the way of Christmas presents for their children this year, and I heard his mother was delighted to see her younger boy, Stefan, getting your sweater." Jenny was thrilled to hear this. She really hoped Stefan would get great use of his new jumper, and especially at this freezing cold time of the year in Romania!

Jenny then remembered Christmas Day itself, which she'd spent at Ricky and Lisa's, her brother and sister-in-law's, along with her parents and little niece Amy, Ricky and Lisa's daughter. Amy was now nine months old and as her teeth were starting to emerge, she'd spent most of the day chewing on baby rusks or sinking her jaws into nearby objects, especially ones at floor level! A few small wisps of red hair had also started to sprout on the top of her head, not unlike the colour of her father's at the same age!

Carole and Tracey had also arrived in the evening, when Tracey had talked about her medical elective in Sudan, including details about little Yaya. She reported, "I got an email from the Camp Director on Christmas Eve, who mentioned that Yaya has safely returned to her village and that volunteers from a Scottish charity are arriving in the New Year to build new homes in her village. The rains have also arrived and many villagers, including Yaya's family, have started to plant crops such as sweet potatoes and beans. No doubt Yaya would find her small knitted sweater most useful in the cooler evenings, whilst she helped her mother to harvest their crops!"

After everyone had tucked into Lisa's ham and cheese sandwiches, plus some Marks & Spencer Christmas cake, there was time to sit down and watch one of the Christmas movies. Jenny remembered she'd brought Auntie Sue's little pattern with her, plus the extra balls of wool she'd purchased in town, and took the opportunity to start a bit more knitting! In no time, another small sweater was almost complete. Jenny planned to finish it during her New Year weekend break, and maybe get another one started with the remaining wool she'd bought! Two small sweaters might come in useful for future appeals.

In the meantime, she'd come to Ikea to buy a new bed. Since Steve died, she'd slept in their large double bed in the main bedroom, but the mattress had since started to sag, and she needed to buy a replacement.

As Jenny walked through Ikea's main entrance, then travelled up the elevator with a couple of twin boys and their grandfather in front, it didn't take long to reach the bedroom furniture section on the first floor. She quietly reminded herself that she'd a limited budget to spend, as she stood and gazed at the huge range of beds and mattresses on display. A friendly sales assistant with the name "Gillian" printed on her badge quickly approached Jenny.

"Can I help you, Madam?" she asked. "I expect you're looking for a mattress for your husband and yourself." Jenny gave a slight gulp. It was a bit like the time she'd been asked an awkward question by Pearl at the knitting workshop.

"Actually, I'm looking for a mattress for myself," Jenny quietly replied. She didn't want to start explaining that she was a young widow as Gillian slightly blushed and apologised for her question.

Gillian continued, "I think we should have what you're looking for, Madam. Would you kindly fill in this small questionnaire?" She then handed Jenny a free Ikea pen to complete the questionnaire. After recording her sleeping position, preferred firmness of mattress and choice of bed base, Gillian quickly glanced at Jenny's answers then directed her to a couple of bed frames and mattresses that seemed to tick the right boxes. "I suggest this deep pocket-sprung mattress plus the oak-framed bed base seems a wise choice." Jenny agreed and filled in the barcode numbers on her order form. She quickly decided these were enough to purchase at the moment although she did spot a few pretty pillowcases and duvet covers.

A few minutes later, Jenny left the bedroom furniture section and headed to the marketplace on the ground floor. After a bit of a trek she reached the exit tills and paid for her new purchases with her Visa Debit card. She also arranged for their delivery the following Saturday, her next day off.

Jenny glanced down at her watch and noticed it was now 12.30pm. She thought, "I'm starting to feel a bit peckish," and remembered there was a nice open-plan café on the first floor, so decided to stay for a quick snack lunch. It didn't take long to climb back upstairs to the café, which overlooked the runway of George Best Airport, just outside Belfast City.

Jenny queued up and bought a portion of meatballs and rice, and a café latte, then headed over to a vacant table overlooking the runway before someone else did. As Jenny started to tuck into her meal, she looked outside and spotted a plane heading from the airport terminal towards the end of the runway. She suddenly put down her knife and fork as a distant memory came into her head...

She was ten-year-old Jenny again, watching her Aunt Sue's plane taking off from Aldergrove Airport at the beginning of her Vietnam Trip. Jenny couldn't keep her eyes off the plane as it got ready for take-off, then a few moments later, roared down the runway and disappeared into the clouds. Jenny knew this memory of Auntie Sue's Trip had inspired her as a ten-year-old girl to learn more about the world and to do something useful with her life. It also challenged her to think about nursing as a future career. Jenny couldn't believe that she was now 28 years old, a working nurse, and had also learnt to knit!

A few moments later, Jenny was startled as she heard a familiar voice behind her. "Hi, it's Jenny, isn't it?" the voice asked. Jenny turned around and smiled as she noticed the pretty coloured scarf, which she'd seen before.

"You're Pearl, aren't you?" Jenny asked.

Pearl replied, "You're right. If I remember, you're Jenny! You were with your friend Carole at the knitting workshop in the library and I loved the little sweater you were making. No doubt you've already put it to good use. Perhaps you've even knitted some more!"

Jenny smiled in return. "I've already completed two small sweaters, and I'm just about to finish two more! I sewed one of your little motifs onto each one."

"How lovely," responded Pearl. "Some small children will really appreciate these."

Jenny continued, "I know I'll probably never meet the kids who received them, but it's still nice to hear their news." Jenny briefly told Pearl what she'd heard about little Yaya in Sudan and Stefan in Romania. Pearl was really interested to hear their stories as she placed her handbag under the table and sat down opposite Jenny. She also got a compliment herself.

"I see you've finished your scarf," said Jenny. "It's gorgeous and beautifully knitted! You're certainly a great model for your work!"

Pearl chuckled. "Glad you like it," she responded. "I only got it finished last week and wore it on Christmas Day when the rest of the family were around. In fact, my sister liked it so much that she now wants me to knit one for her!"

Jenny grinned. "Pearl, I wouldn't mind one myself!"

"Well, Jenny," Pearl replied. "If you come back to the next knitting workshop, I'll think about making that happen!"

Jenny continued, "I might get back one of these days if my boss stops putting me on Tuesday evening rotas. It's nice to have a bit of a hobby outside my main job."

"Great!" responded Pearl. "Marie's hoping to share some special ideas from her recent craft trip in Peru at the next workshop."

"I must remember that," said Jenny. "I'll put the date in my diary."

Pearl then quietly muttered, "This place seems really busy today. I only called to look at the range of kids' beds."

"I didn't know you'd young kids, Pearl," said Jenny.

"No, I don't," replied Pearl. "My Simon's nineteen and gone off to uni in England, but I'm looking at kids' beds as I'm offering short term respite to a couple of young Syrian girls. They're arriving next week as asylum seekers from the war out there and I'm going to put their beds in Simon's old room. I believe they've come from Aleppo and lost virtually everything after the recent attacks in their city. They've been staying in a large French refugee camp in Calais for the past five weeks, after walking for miles through Europe and enduring a rough sea crossing from some beach on the North African coast."

Jenny responded, "Poor kids. They'll be shattered after all that. I'm sure they'll be really glad of your hospitality, Pearl."

Pearl then continued, "Mike, my husband, is doing some volunteering work at a drop-in centre in South Belfast where asylum seekers and refugees come to get advice or practical support. In a couple of weeks, he's flying to Paris, then travelling on to Calais with a few other centre volunteers, to support more refugees in one of the temporary camps. They're also taking out a range of extra donated goods as extra baggage. Mike and his friends have already set up an appeal at the drop-in centre for blankets, small toys, and sweaters for adults and children. I'm going to donate a knitted blanket and a few small sweaters to this collection point myself."

Jenny was touched by this and responded, "I'd like to donate something too. These folks must have lived through some terrible nightmares." Pearl nodded as she opened her handbag and placed a copy of a local paper on the table. The front page reported a huge massacre in one of the Syrian cities called Aleppo, where the day before hundreds of people had been injured plus a huge number killed. Many had to flee their homes and run for their lives. Pearl didn't want to share all the details with Jenny but knew these facts were likely to be true as Mike had already told her stories that he'd been told by some of the Syrian refugees at the drop-in centre. He'd mentioned a number of women and children had been hit by a chemical attack and that all the Aleppo hospitals were now at crisis point. Many refugees had also travelled to Lebanon or Turkey for safety, but sadly a number of young men and boys had been captured or murdered on the way.

Jenny sat in silence for a few moments before she spoke. "Pearl, I've been thinking. I'd like to donate a small knitted sweater that I'm about to finish to Mike's drop-in centre appeal. I'll even sew one of your small motifs onto the front!" Pearl replied, "That would be great, Jenny. If you don't mind, you'll need to deliver it by Tuesday week, when it will be packed up for the journey to Calais."

A short while later, the two ladies finished lunch and Pearl headed off to Sainsbury's garage nearby to get some petrol before heading home, whilst Jenny glanced out the window at another plane that was about to take off on the runway. As this made her think again about her Auntie Sue taking small sweaters on her trips to faraway places, she was also aware of how blessed she was to live in a cosy house with a solid roof, a warm bed each night, water at the turn of a tap, and a flush toilet that worked. She knew many displaced people in the world were surviving in makeshift camps far from home, with little food, freezing cold weather and almost non-existent sanitation, as they escaped the horrors of war or famine either inside or out of their country.

The following Saturday soon arrived. Jenny quickly answered the door when she saw the large Ikea delivery van parked outside her house with her new bed and mattress on board. It didn't take long for the delivery men to unload these items and carry them to Jenny's main bedroom upstairs. Before long, Jenny had the new bed covered with clean sheets and pillows. A comfortable night's sleep was in order! Before heading downstairs, Jenny walked over to the spare bedroom and opened the door of the small wardrobe where she'd left her knitting bag the evening before. She lifted out her latest almost-completed small sweater, plus the remaining motifs that Pearl gave her at the knitting workshop. As Jenny gently held a small smiley-faced motif in her hand, she decided she'd sew it onto her latest small sweater if she managed to finish it that evening. The tiny smile looked like a little bit of hope…

Jenny got her sweater finished. On the following Monday morning she left it at Mike's drop-in centre as a donation for the refugees in Calais.

CHAPTER NINE

JAMIRAH'S STORY (SYRIA)

Jenny enjoyed hearing some of Mike's stories after his trip to Calais with a few of the other drop-in centre volunteers when he called around for supper with Pearl later on during a Saturday night in January. They'd spent most of their time at a large Refugee Camp called "The Jungle," where they donated the goods brought from Belfast were delivered to, and also helped out at a soup kitchen and a makeshift school in the Camp. Most of the folks in the camp had arrived from Iraq or Syria by an overland makeshift bus journey across Europe and an earlier sea crossing via the Turkish or Greek coast. Many of the refugees had lost family members in the war or got separated on their journey to Europe, where they'd hoped to find safety and peace.

Mike reported, "Some the younger children looked really frail and cold and had only one set of damaged clothes, so I helped to sort and distribute some warm woolly clothes plus shoes for these kids. One little girl received a small red sweater with a sun on the front. If I remember correctly, this was the sweater you kindly donated yourself."

Jenny nodded her head to confirm this then had quietly asked, "Did you get any details about this little girl?"

"Yes, I did," Mike responded. "One of the Syrian interpreters told me she was called Jamirah and came from Aleppo in Syria. She'd arrived at the Calais camp the day before I did, along with her parents and younger brothers, and had a difficult story to tell…"

Jamirah's home was Aleppo where she loved playing with her friends, especially her best friend, Rima, who lived nearby. The girls were in the same class at school and both loved painting and geography, where they'd learnt about other countries in the world, including the ones near their own. Jamirah had also enjoyed visiting her cousins in Homs during the school holidays, a city some miles away. At weekends, Jamirah's family worshipped in a small Christian church although many of the neighbours, like Rima's family, were Muslims. All the neighbours had got on well and looked out for each other, especially in the summer months when it got really hot.

But things changed. Jamirah's school bus had been frequently cancelled in the mornings, and no one stayed out late at night anymore. Some men and boys from Aleppo had suddenly disappeared, including two boys from Jamirah's class at school. She'd also noticed her father, Nabil, had started to come home late from work several nights a week. His small computer hardware store in Aleppo was losing customers and he looked more tense and strained as each day passed.

One day Jamirah asked her mum, Zeinah, if she could visit Rima's house. Zeinah hesitated before answering. "No Jamirah, I'm not going to let you go today. It's too... too... dangerous." She had seemed anxious, but Zeinah wasn't normally like that.

The following evening, after going to bed, Jamirah had heard her father Nabil speaking downstairs. "Four families have left the neighbourhood this week. The Ossmans have gone to Homs, the Sammans have gone to Jordan to stay with friends. I think we need to prepare for the worst..."

Jamirah didn't like her father saying these things. She didn't want to leave her home and not go to school to see her friends. Later on that week, her world in Aleppo changed forever...

Jamirah had been almost asleep in bed when she'd heard a large bang, sounds of gunfire and the noise of people running outside. She glanced out the window and saw several neighbours carrying plastic bags and blankets. Some didn't have shoes on their feet and many seemed to be crying.

Before she could think any further, her father, Nabil, had rushed into the room, carrying Farid her youngest brother in his arms, whilst Mahdi, her other brother, gripped onto Nabil's arm. Both boys looked as if they'd just been dragged out of bed.

Jamirah remembered her father saying, "Hurry, Jamirah. Get out of bed and quickly put on your outdoor clothes and leather shoes," as he threw her a cardigan and small jacket which were lying on a chair. Jamirah tried to find her nice leather shoes, but could only see her soft cloth slippers, so put them on instead.

"Quick, Jamirah," Nabil continued. "There's no time to lose." Jamirah had then started to feel really frightened. She knew she was leaving her home, but hopefully not for long. She hadn't even time to pack her crayons or favourite doll. What happened next was worse…

The whole family ran out of the front door and through the arched gateway with only a small bag of food and a few extra pieces of clothing between them. There was no time to grab anything else. As they joined up with a large crowd of other neighbours Jamirah asked her Dad where they were going.

"I don't know," Nabil had replied, "We've got to keep moving. We're getting out of Aleppo." Jamirah didn't like the sound of this at all. She wanted the comfort of her familiar surroundings and friends.

Suddenly, the crowd were stopped in their tracks. Several large trucks drove into the area with flags flying from their roofs as uniformed men with cloth head coverings jumped out of the trucks, throwing grenades into the crowd and firing guns into the air. Several young men and boys were rounded up and forced into the trucks, which were then driven away a few minutes later. Jamirah recognised one of the captured boys as a friend of Rima's older brother.

Jamirah's family and the rest of the terrified crowd walked on towards the suburbs of Aleppo, whilst gunfire was heard in the distance and bright flares of light glowed in the dark. Some of the smaller children struggled to keep up with the crowd with several starting to cry from hunger and thirst.

Eventually, the moving crowd reached a small village with large flags flying on a number of the buildings. Several houses were damaged, but a tiny shop still stood open in the centre of the village with a blown off roof and small birds flying in and out of gaps in the walls.

Suddenly the crowd heard the sound of sniper bullets near-by and rushed into this building for emergency shelter, which included running down an uneven set of stone steps towards a basement cellar. As they all squeezed into the confined space in the basement, tiredness and exhaustion set in, but no one actually slept. The temperature had dropped to almost zero degrees and everyone shivered with cold. There was no proper toilet around and many of the small babies in the group cried loudly, in urgent need of a feed or nappy change. Jamirah also noticed that some of the men had cuts on their hands and faces. Jamirah lost track of time...

The following morning as dawn arrived, there was a loud noise outside the building and shouting voices as masked men carrying weapons entered the building and told the whole group they had to leave. Everyone was forced to start walking again, including Jamirah's family. Zeinah held tightly onto Farid and Jamirah's hands as Nabil and Madhi kept close behind.

Whilst they walked out of the village, Jamirah noticed some other children who'd nasty burns on their skin. She later heard they'd been injured in a chemical attack at their school in Aleppo, not far from her own. This was terrible news. Some of the adults talked about family members who'd gone to Jordan or Lebanon for safety but hadn't been heard of since.

Jamirah turned and asked her mother a question, "When are we going back to Aleppo? My feet are sore and my stomach's starting to rumble. I told Rima I would call at her house next week. I don't want to miss her birthday."

Zeinah stared ahead with sad eyes. "I don't think we'll see Rima for a very long time. We're going on a long journey to a place where we're we'll feel safer. Rima will be OK. She'll be thinking about you when you're away."

Jamirah then heard a small child sobbing near her side. It was Farid. He was thirsty and tired and wanted to go home... Everyone wanted to go home...

A short time later, a convoy of lorries appeared in the distance. Jamirah and the others slowly made their way towards them whilst their teeth chattered in the cold and their bodies ached all over. When the crowd reached the lorries, they spotted people handing out bread rolls and bottles of water before they were forced to get onto a lorry. As the drivers of the vehicles started up the engines and quickly drove off, no one from Aleppo knew where they were going or when they were likely to stop. The next part of their journey would take several weeks...

Jamirah remembered stopping at the Syrian border, where a few rough looking men got onto her vehicle, then some Turkish flags outside many houses in the villages they drove through. Eventually, the lorry drew to a halt at the top of a steep hill just before the sun set one evening with what looked like a dense forest nearby. Almost immediately the sight and sound of an approaching vehicle was heard, which turned out to be a jeep with blackened windows and large tyres. Several men and a couple of women jumped out of the jeep and started to hand out lifejackets.

Mike continued as Jenny and Pearl listened to the further nightmare details that were shared by Jamirah's interpreter...

Jamirah clung onto her father's hand as everyone was told to stay quiet and to start walking down the steep slope. She also told the interpreter, "There was a full moon that night and I saw water glistening on a beach in the distance with big inflatable dinghies bobbing in the tide. After reaching the bottom of the hill, everyone was squashed like sardines into four big rubber dinghies with several patched holes on each side. I could hardly cling onto the edge of my dinghy and my lifejacket was far too large. Farid didn't get a lifejacket at all as there weren't enough for the smaller children. Then a few of the rough looking men from the jeeps jumped into the dinghies. Mine nearly tipped over as everyone got pushed onto the starboard side and one of the fierce men reached the controls. As my dinghy was then quickly steered out into the rough, choppy sea beyond the calmer part of the beach I was really frightened and could hardly get a breath. I knew I couldn't swim and was scared I'd lose my family. Suddenly I was pushed into the sea where the water felt freezing and waves rolled over my head. Then there was darkness..."

Jamirah remembered waking up someplace with lots of tents. It was Calais, in France, but she didn't know that for a while. At least all her family were still alive and together and had been offered a tiny, cramped tent to live in. All of them were thin, tired and weak and Jamirah noticed her mother Zeinah still wore the same cloth skirt and jacket that she'd quickly put on when she'd left Aleppo. Poor Mahdi also seemed to have caught a fever.

Jamirah said, "I burst into tears with relief when the family of one of my school friends got a small tent nearby. They must have escaped from Aleppo about the same time as us." At least the girls were pleased to see each other but couldn't help thinking about their other friends back in Syria.

Jamirah also shared, "Lots of kind volunteer people have come to our tents and given out special T-shirts and fleeces, although they speak a language I don't understand. They also brought food boxes, soap, blankets and cooking pots to families like mine. There was rice, oil, biscuits, tea, dried peas and small cans of meat in the boxes. Other workers came and gave us heaters and fuel. We were all happy to receive this help. I also got a small toy, some colouring pencils, a hat and a knitted sweater. Mahdi and Farid each got a pair of socks and a small notebook, but I really love my red sweater and it keeps me warm. I would like to thank the person who made it and especially for putting the little smiley face on the front. It makes me feel happy."

Jenny knew this was the sweater she had made, and was glad Mike had shared this story.

Mike then continued, "A small school has been set up in the Camp, including a nursery for the very young children. Zeinah and some of the other ladies are now making new clothes and many of the refugee men like Nabil are starting to learn new skills like making furniture or baking bread so they can try to get a job in the future. Some have already started to grow root vegetables after being given seeds and spades."

Jenny was so happy to hear about Jamirah receiving her small red sweater. Someday she might return to Aleppo and be able to show it to her friends like Rima. Overall, Jenny was glad Mike and the other drop-in centre volunteers had visited the Calais camp. She was thrilled another of her small sweaters had given hope and comfort to another young child...

CHAPTER TEN

THE MEXICO TEAM AT CHURCH

Jenny enjoyed having a well-earned weekend off work, staying with Ricky, Lisa and Amy at their cottage in the village of Helens Bay at the edge of Belfast Lough. The house used to belong to Jenny and Ricky's grandparents, but when they got older and found it too expensive to maintain, Ricky and Lisa had decided to buy it as a future investment. They'd recently made it into a larger family home, including a nice conservatory that overlooked the Lough.

Jenny gazed out the window as Lisa walked into the room and tried to steer Amy away from their small family French bulldog called Oscar, who looked as if his ears might get pulled any minute. "I always loved coming here when Gran was around," Jenny said. "I remember the house as a wee quaint dwelling set back from the road, and I know Auntie Sue often stayed after coming back from one of her mercy trips. It must have been a great place for her to knit her little sweaters!"

"That's right, Jenny," Lisa responded, "Ricky told me the same. I know Oscar's happy it's close to the beach for his afternoon walks, and there's plenty of room for Amy to spread her wings — not that she's a little angel all the time!"

Jenny smiled and nodded in agreement as Amy, almost a year old now, reminded Jenny of what Ricky was like at the same age, a little livewire who'd started to crawl and no doubt would be walking anytime soon.

"I must get a move on, as I'm hoping to go to Church with you this morning. I know you'll probably want to go early to give Amy time to settle in the Creche."

Lisa responded, "No problem, Jenny. Grannie Valerie is planning to pop over for lunch later on, and no doubt she'll enjoy keeping Any amused this afternoon!"

The small church itself stood proudly in the village not far from Ricky and Lisa's cottage, surrounded by neat grass and a few pretty flowerbeds with snowdrops sprouting in the soil. Jenny had often attended Sunday morning worship whilst staying with her grandparents during school holidays. It wasn't long before it was time to head over to the church as Lisa safely tucked Amy into her buggy and put a small favourite toy in her hand, whilst Jenny put on a warm scarf and pair of gloves. Ricky wanted to join them but agreed to follow a few minutes later, as he needed to check a small leak that seemed to have appeared in the garage.

"It never rains but it pours, as they say in "Norn Ireland", and it certainly does in this house," Ricky muttered. "I dread to think where the next leak will start. Last time it was the gutter above the conservatory roof and before that the sink in the up-stairs bathroom. The joys of living in an old cottage!" Jenny and Lisa gave a laugh as they listened but still headed for the front door. At least they were going to arrive at the church in good time, well before eleven o'clock, and should be able to get a good seat near the front of the congregation.

When Lisa, Jenny and Amy arrived at the Church a short stroll later, Lisa took Amy to the crèche based in a small hall at the rear of the main building, whilst Jenny entered the main church foyer. It was great to see so many familiar faces. Several folks who'd called at Jenny's home in Belfast with small gifts of food or flowers after Steve died still remembered her, and greeted her warmly as she headed towards the front of the sanctuary. A few minutes later, Lisa joined Jenny after settling Amy at the crèche and was then followed by Ricky, who arrived just as the first hymn started. The service got underway, and Jenny loved watching the faces of the small children who came up to the front of the congregation during the short talk for the children. Shortly after this, the collection was gathered in, before Rev. Shaw, the preacher, walked over to the small pulpit at the front and read out a portion of Scripture.

"Today's reading is from Acts chapter 9, verses 36–43," he announced as he waited for his parishioners to look up the passage should they wish to follow it as he read:

"In Joppa there was a disciple named Tabitha (which, when translated, is Dorcas), who was always doing good and helping the poor. About that time, she became sick and died, and her body was washed and placed in an upstairs room. Lydda was near Joppa; so when the disciples heard that Peter was in Lydda, they sent two men to him and urged him, "Please come at once!"

Peter went with them, and when he arrived, he was taken upstairs to the room. All the widows stood around him, crying and showing him the robes and other clothing that Dorcas had made while she was still with them. Peter sent them all out of the room; then he got down on his knees and prayed. Turning towards the dead woman, he said, "Tabitha, get up." She opened her eyes, and, seeing Peter, she sat up. He took her by the hand and helped her to her feet. Then he called the believers and the widows and presented her to them alive. This became known all over Joppa, and many people believed in the Lord. Peter stayed in Joppa for some time with a tanner called Simon.

Jenny was delighted that this passage was about a lady who had used her talent of making clothes to help others in need and had also been a widow like herself. She'd obviously put her faith into action, and "walked the talk" despite the circumstances of her life. Jenny thought this reading was very appropriate, as she knew her own life seemed to have taken an unexpected turn, but there had to be a purpose in it all.

Shortly after the reading, Rev. Shaw announced that a small group of young people from the congregation were planning to travel to Mexico in three weeks' time, and invited them to the front to share some details of their forthcoming Trip. They all looked around 20-25 years old and seemed really enthusiastic about their forthcoming adventure.

The team consisted of Sandy, a student teacher, Beth, a radiography student, Stacey, a dental nurse, Roy, a trainee engineer, James, a civil servant, and Paul, a sports medicine student.

Sandy spoke first. She explained the Team were planning to travel from Dublin to Mexico City via Amsterdam, spending their first week at a large orphanage just outside Mexico City. During the next two weeks, they hoped to be involved in a range of activities, including organising a kids' club and volunteering at a small football academy in an impoverished township.

Stacey, who looked more like eighteen years old than twenty-four, planned to help a local dentist set up a mobile dental clinic, and Beth aimed to link up with a local priest who'd a ministry issuing food parcels and gifts to needy township families. Some of these families would be facing illness or unemployment, and several might have a relative in prison.

Roy, who looked about six-foot-tall, and Paul, the sports medicine student, then stepped forward. Roy explained, "We'll be doing some coaching at the football academy for young boys. Few of these boys would have had the chance to go to school, and many are at risk of being lured into gangs where they can end up sniffing glue or taking drugs and living on the streets. These boys have often run away from home to escape poverty or a violent family member."

James, the civil servant, who looked the oldest of the other team members, then shared more information. "I plan to help Sandy with the kids' club, including painting some wall murals and making balloon puppets with the kids!"

Finally, Sandy, the teacher, added some extra details. "All the team are bringing extra goods in our luggage. If anyone wants to donate any soft toys, small T-shirts and even small jumpers, we'd be most grateful!"

Jenny especially noted the request for jumpers! The little sweater she'd finished just after New Year could go to this appeal. It would also be a practical way of showing her own faith in action.

A few moments later, the Mexico Team members returned to their seats, as the Rev. Shaw stepped forward to deliver a sermon. He included points about showing love in action as highlighted in the earlier Bible Reading from the book of Acts. Jenny knew her latest small sweater could help to demonstrate this goal! After Rev. Shaw stopped preaching, there was one further hymn, then the service came to an end.

At that point Lisa stood up and muttered to Jenny, "You're welcome to come with me to the crèche to get Amy. Ricky's going to head home now, as Valerie might have already arrived." It wasn't often the family had a get-together, and this weekend was particularly special as Ricky was celebrating his school promotion, and also Lisa's birthday.

After collecting Amy, who seemed to have enjoyed her time in the crèche, Jenny and Lisa also walked back to the house. When they arrived, Grannie Valerie was already there and had almost completed preparations for lunch.

"I'd recognise your good cookin' anywhere, Mum, especially the smell of your roast potatoes," Ricky called out as he walked into the kitchen.

Valerie responded, "Thanks! Lunch is ready! You can help me carry these dishes into the dining room!"

Ricky helped his mother to lift the cooked food trays and heated plates from of the oven and carry them into the dining room. Amy's highchair had already been positioned between Granny Valerie's and her Mum's, with Jenny seated on the other side of the table.

"I think you've got the best spot, Jenny," said Lisa. "Amy might throw a few spoonfuls of food onto your lap, but if she misses, Oscar will be happy to catch the remains under the table!" Oscar was already lying patiently on the carpet, waiting for some morsel of food to land his way!

It didn't take long to gobble up Valerie's chicken and broccoli bake, plus her roast potatoes and veg, followed by the strawberry pavlova from the fridge. Whilst everyone finished their meal, including Amy, who was now happily chewing a rusk between her gums, Valerie walked across the room to her handbag and lifted out a small bundle of old photographs, before carrying them back to the table. Jenny took a quick glance at the first photo and quickly recognised the scene.

"Do you know where that was taken?" Valerie asked Jenny, as Jenny nodded.

"It's not hard to guess," she responded. "I think it's Auntie Sue outside a small clinic in Vietnam. I recognise the T-shirts and straw hats! No doubt she made the little knitted sweaters that some of the kids are wearing!" Jenny then passed the photograph to Ricky.

"I remember this too!" he said. "I think Auntie Sue knitted those jumpers when she was here at the cottage! I remember some of her wool got tangled and I helped to her sort it out!" Jenny and Valerie continued to browse through the rest of the photos as Ricky and Lisa then got up to clear the dishes, and Oscar quietly munched a dog chew under the table! When Lisa returned, she took Amy upstairs for a short nap. By now it was almost three o'clock.

"I think I'd better take Oscar for a short walk," said Ricky as he got up from the table. "Good idea," said Valerie, "If you don't mind, I'll not join you, as I think I could do with a short doze for a while." She then headed upstairs whilst Jenny agreed to join Ricky and Oscar for their short walk on Helens Bay beach. Jenny called up to Lisa to let her know that she was joining Ricky on the dog walk then headed to the cloakroom to collect her coat and scarf. The weather was fairly cloudy and mild for the time of year, so she decided not to bring a hat.

As Ricky clipped Oscar's lead onto his collar, he gave a short bark and began to head for the door, as he couldn't wait for his walk on the beach! Ricky and Jenny quickly put on their coats and followed Oscar outside. It didn't take long to reach the path that ran along the main beach. Several other family groups or individuals had the same idea and were also walking their dogs. Oscar seemed quite happy on his shorter lead, although several other dogs were running freely into the pounding waves on the shore.

Jenny turned and spoke to Ricky as they listened to the sounds of the sea, "I really enjoyed the service today, and I was really inspired by all those young people going to Mexico City."

Ricky agreed. "I was too. All of them were former pupils at my school. It's great they're so enthusiastic and excited about going on their mission trip. Michael, who's now an engineer, used to come to the Church youth club for a while, and I know Sandy and Beth loved helping in the Creche. Roy and Paul will be a great help at the football academy, as football is just their thing. They were always kicking a ball around the school playground at break times. My school's already started to collect some of the items that the team requested at the service today. Lisa is gathering up the donated goods in our garage."

Jenny responded. "I wish I could contribute something, but I'm afraid I don't have any exciting T-shirts or small shoes to offer you at the moment. I could give you a donation of money."

"That would certainly help," commented Ricky. "Every penny counts."

As the chat continued, a small dog ran past and headed towards the beach to catch a small ball. He seemed full of life and really enjoying the moment. This inspired Jenny with an idea.

"Ricky," she asked, "Do you remember those small sweaters that Auntie Sue used to knit, like the ones in the photo at lunchtime? You'll have a laugh, but I've recently started to knit myself. I found one of Auntie Sue's old patterns in my attic and subsequently went off to join a local knitting workshop! Mind you, there was more nattering than knitting at the class, but I did learn a few tips."

Ricky had a cheeky grin on his face as he then commented, "I'm sure you'd no problem with the nattering, there's times when you never stop talking! However, you're not a bad Sis, Jen. You've always looked out for me and now I want to look out for you. Seriously, I often worry about you and know things haven't been easy for a while."

"Thanks Ricky," Jenny quietly responded. "I know you'll always be there for me. I want to support Lisa, Amy and yourself if you ever need me."

As they walked on with Oscar pulling at his lead, Ricky shared a bit of information. "I think Lisa's got a bit of the knitting bug herself. She's already knitted a couple of small cardigans for the Mexico Team."

Just as Ricky said this, Jenny looked at him and spoke. "I've thought of something. I sewed a small football motif onto the last small sweater I knitted from Auntie Sue's pattern and could donate it to the Mexico Team's collection for one of the kids at the football academy." Ricky agreed this was a great idea.

Ricky and Jenny continued their beach walk with Oscar for another half hour then headed back to the cottage. They wanted to see their Mum before she left before tea, and Jenny also needed get back on the road not too late as she was on duty the following morning...

Jenny called at Ricky and Lisa's on the following Wednesday evening to leave in a small box of biscuits as a gift, as well as her small sweater with the football motif on the front. Oscar was delighted to see her and more than happy to sample one of her biscuits! Jenny looked forward to hearing how the Mexico City Team fared, and especially about what happened to her little sweater...

CHAPTER ELEVEN

JOSÉ'S STORY (MEXICO CITY)

José loved to dream. "I wish I could be a famous footballer like the ones on TV during the World Cup," José muttered to his mother, Maria, and baby brother, Miguel, as Maria swept the floor of their small home perched on a steep hillside in a poor area of Mexico City called a barrio, in Tepito, near one of the city's rubbish dumps.

"Maybe that will happen someday, José," said Maria, "But for now I need you to help me with our market stall and I've no money to pay for football training. Maybe if your Dad hadn't been killed down the copper mine it might be different, but I'm the main family earner now and I've got to make a living for Miguel and yourself." José's Dad had been killed deep below ground with twenty other miners in Chile, after a small earth tremor caused rocks to fall in the area where they'd been working. All these miners had been fathers so other children had also lost their dads. José really wished a miracle had happened when his father died, and that all the trapped miners had got rescued instead.

José liked to help his mother at their market stall in Tepito, but he would really rather go to school, where lots of boys his age were taught to read and write, received a good meal, and could even learn to play football. José knew footballers earned lots of money, and he wouldn't mind that happening to him! His Dad, Francisco, had been great at playing football himself, but didn't get the chance to develop this skill further as he'd become a miner when he was only sixteen, and needed to travel to Chile for work.

"If I was a rich footballer, I'd be able to buy a nice house for you and Miguel, and we could move to the part of Mexico City with the big shops and nice government buildings," José announced, even though this was most highly unlikely. At the moment his small home was basically a small apartment, with a tiny kitchen and one bedroom that doubled up as a living room, too. The house had only two windows covered by small bars and shutters, and the creaky front door swung on small metal hinges. The roof wasn't properly finished and sprouted large metal prongs which stuck into the sky. This meant the owners didn't have to pay as much tax to the government, which saved a lot of money! José's home also didn't have running water or a proper toilet and at night he slept on a small mat on the floor, whilst Miguel dozed on a blanket nearby. Maria had to make do with their small rickety sofa as a bed.

"Mum, I really want to go to school very soon, even if I can't play football. I don't like all the steep paths and rickety steps on the way to the market everyday and I'm a bit scared of the wild pigs and stray dogs that scavenge in the rubbish! Ugh!" On the main road not far from the market, Maria and José often had to walk past tons of sewage that included rotting food or needed to step through puddles of filthy water. If sewage flowed near José's house, which it frequently did, Maria had to walk to a local pump to get water to flush the waste away. During the evenings when rubbish bags were left out for refuge collection, wild dogs sometimes arrived and bit into the bags, spilling the contents onto the path nearby. José felt bad when he frequently saw Miguel's old nappies being blown down the street on windier days, after the wild dogs had ripped the bags apart.

During weekdays, Miguel was left with a neighbour called Juana, who looked after him until Maria and José got home in the evenings. Sometimes on Saturdays José went to a small boys' club at a little Church in the barrio, where there were games and lots of stories, including some from the Bible. Maria let him go there, as he loved meeting the other kids and listening to the stories at the club, especially the ones about miracles, and on Sundays Maria also attended the small church.

Now it was Monday, one of the days when José and Maria had to leave very early in the morning to get to the market. "Hurry up, José," called Maria. "Eat your tortilla and banana, and make sure Miguel has his. We're going to be late if we don't get organised!"

After a few minutes, they'd all eaten. Maria checked Miguel had no stains on his clean T-shirt, whilst José put some small hessian sacks and display baskets into a large cloth bag, then they all left home for the day. First of all, they left Miguel at Juana's, then Maria and José walked to another nearby barrio to collect produce for their stall. On the way to the market they chatted.

"Can I have tacos and a spicy tortilla pancake for lunch today?" José asked.

Maria gave a sigh as she answered. "Of course you can, José, but we'll need to sell plenty of fruit and vegetables to get enough money to buy them. Don't forget to cover our stall with a large cloth in the afternoon to stop the hot sun destroying our goods." José agreed this was a good idea, as the weather was particularly hot at the moment and they didn't want their produce to get ruined. At this time of year, they usually sold sweet potatoes, chilli beans, squashes, carrots, tomatoes and peppers plus some tropical fruits such as melons, limes, oranges and pineapples. José loved to look at all their pretty colours when they were on display, and sometimes Maria allowed him to kick a watermelon around like a football if there was one was left at the end of the day!

Thankfully, on most days Maria and José sold the produce on their stall. If there were any unsold vegetables, they brought a little home for themselves, or sometimes gave a spare tomato or carrot to one of the street boys begging near the market entrance. Maria warned José to be careful when he was near these boys.

"Don't get caught up with them," she warned. "They often move about in small gangs and get into trouble. Some even try to steal money or jewellery from people at the market or when walking along the pavements." Maria was afraid of José getting caught up with these boys, as many sniffed glue or tried to take drugs.

"I wish we were at the market now," uttered José as he shuffled behind Maria through the early morning smog. "My feet are getting sore."

Maria quickly replied, "Stop complaining José. At least you've got shoes on your feet. My legs often swell in the heat whilst I'm standing for hours at our stall. When I was your age, I didn't have shoes at all." José had to admit he was glad he had shoes, even if they were only cheap training ones with mismatching laces, and also because his mother had only a pair of flat sandals to stop her own feet getting painful. Maria was wearing a long loose skirt and T shirt, with her long, shiny black hair tied into a ponytail, like many other ladies who also ran stalls at the market, as she slowly walked in front of José carrying the large cloth bag filled with smaller hessian bags. On some evenings, whilst walking home, José felt a big chilly as the sum disappeared into the evening smog. He often imagined it would be lovely to get a nice warm sweater or tunic from somewhere, but Maria could never afford to buy him one.

About an hour later, Maria and José reached Tepito market to set up their stall. As early customers began to arrive, José helped to set out a range of fruit and vegetables into the hessian bags or baskets that they'd brought from home. Local farmers and growers had already left their produce in large boxes at the market early that morning, and many had known Maria for several years.

Soon the morning sales got underway.

"Good price! I give you good price!" Maria exclaimed to several customers as they tried to bargain for their fruit and veg, particularly for the chillies and sweet potatoes that were in season. "I just ask for four dollars. A bargain today!" José was amused at the tough bargaining of some customers who only wanted a cheap deal, particularly the ones who looked like they'd plenty of cash to spend!

Soon it was midday. Maria and José had already managed to sell most of their produce and now could do with a rest. Maria turned to José and said, "Why don't you take a small break? I can look after the stall while you go and get something to eat. Here's four pesos. See if you can get me a fajita and a bottle of Sprite. You can also get some for yourself."

José took the coins from Maria, squeezed through the gap at the side of their stall then headed off to find some food. As he walked past several other stalls he was amazed at the variety of goods for sale, everything from jewellery to shoes. He especially loved the stall selling warm jumpers, many of them knitted in bright colours and made from alpaca wool. José knew this wool came from large mountain goats that lived in the high mountains, far away from the large Mexican cities.

Suddenly José spotted a trader called Pedro, who used to live near his own house, and walked over to his stall. "Hi José," called out Pedro. "I haven't seen you for a while. I hope your mother is keeping well. As you can see, I've had a busy morning myself. Most of my meat is already sold, as it's good meat from Argentina."

José then smiled and spoke when he mentioned Argentina. "When I grow up, I want to be a footballer like the ones from Argentina. I know a lot of the good ones are from there. They're my heroes!"

Pedro laughed in response. "I used to want that too but ended up selling meat instead! Don't give up your dreams, José. You never know. You might get an opportunity to become a player yourself. I suppose I'd better not keep you, you'll need to get back to your own stall soon."

José nodded and wished Pedro "Good day," then walked on past a few more stalls. Soon he reached the one that sold fajitas.

José put his hand in his pocket and lifted out the money Maria had given him. He wanted to buy a small taco to take home for Miguel, but there wasn't enough change as he'd just enough for fajitas and two bottles of sprite. Maybe Maria could keep some fruit from their own stall and bring it home to Miguel instead.

José placed his order: "I'd like two hot and spicy fajitas, covered with guacamole sauce, and two small bottles of Sprite lemonade," he requested, as the stallholder wrote down his order on a small writing pad and took the required cash. As José put a small coin back into his pocket, which was loose change, then lifted his purchased food from the stallholder, he suddenly heard a commotion close by. Some street boys had started a fight so José quickly decided he needed to move on. He didn't want to get caught up in any violence where some of the boys could get killed. He felt his own life was worth a lot more. He wanted to be around to support Maria both now and in the future, as she worked hard and tried to give Miguel and himself opportunities that she never had. José ran back to Maria with the fajitas and Sprite as quickly as he could.

"José," exclaimed Maria. "I'm so glad you're here. Some street boys have been walking towards our stall and they looked as if they were going to steal some fruit. It's great you're back and can help me to keep a close eye on things. Thanks for getting the food. I must admit I was starting to feel really hungry myself."

José handed Maria her share, then quickly sank his teeth into his fajita, washing it down with a bottle of sprite lemonade whilst Maria did the same. A couple of minutes later, just as they finished eating, Maria and José noticed a familiar face heading towards their stall. José shouted, "Look, I think it's Eduardo, one the youth leaders who visits our church." Maria nodded in agreement. She also recognised Eduardo and was surprised but pleased to see him. José and Maria knew Eduardo came from a richer part of Mexico City, but didn't seem afraid to meet people from some of the poorer barrios. Eduardo seemed to really care about his poorer neighbours and took an interest in their lives, wanting them to have a good future. José knew Eduardo sometimes offered English lessons for adults, or helped at the homework club in his church, where children from very poor homes could also get a nourishing meal.

Eduardo approached the stall and smiled at José as he spoke. "I've a small gift for you," he said. José looked intrigued. Eduardo lifted up a small plastic bag and handed it to him, telling him that the gift came from a place called Northern Ireland. "I have some friends who are visiting Mexico City for a couple of weeks and coming to volunteer their skills at your church. I know a couple of them are planning to set up a small Football Club and I thought you'd be interested in this!" As Eduardo chatted a bit more, José opened the paper wrapping on the small gift and pulled out the present inside – a lovely red sweater! It matched the bright red peppers on Maria's stall! It also had a football motif on the front, which José thought was really cool!

"That's for you, José," said Eduardo. "I heard you'd love to play football, and thought this would be handy on chilly evenings when you go to football practice!"

José couldn't believe what he saw and was hearing. He couldn't wait to wear his new sweater, and particularly at the new football club when it started. He hoped his other friends at the church youth club would get nice gifts as well.

Maria was delighted when she saw José's new sweater. He'd very few clothes and she often found it hard to get the time or materials to patch up the ones he already had. His two other jumpers were full of holes. Sometimes, in the colder evenings, José had to wear his jumpers all night to keep out the chill he felt in his bones.

Before leaving Maria and José's stall, Eduardo bought some oranges and sweet potatoes, slipping a little extra money into Maria's hand after paying for his goods. He also reminded José that he looked forward to seeing him at the football club in the church.

José could hardly wait for this new adventure. He already knew a lot about football and might even become a great footballing hero himself! Maybe he'd also get the chance to go to school. He'd certainly be wearing his new woolly sweater...

CHAPTER TWELVE

AT THE GYM

"Carole. I think I've had enough of this!" Jenny uttered as she switched off her cross-trainer and gave a huge sigh. "I'm knackered! Ten minutes on this machine is enough! If I don't stop now, I'm going to end up on the floor in a heap!"

Carole quietly chuckled. "Jenny, just look at the state of you! Anyone would think you'd just run a marathon! At least you're still in one piece and in a much better shape than most of the other bodies in this place!" Jenny had to silently agree. A few other gym members looked as if they were well past exhaustion point. Most of the men in the room had spent their time doing weightlifting or exercising on the rowing machines and several of the other females had been doing exercises on floor mats.

A few moments later, Jenny heard a familiar voice behind her. "Hi Jenny. I haven't seen you in ages." Jenny turned around and recognised the tall man standing behind her.

"Hi Andy," she said. "How about you? I see you're still coming to this place. I don't think I've seen you since Steve's funeral."

"That's right, Jenny," Andy quietly replied, "Steve and I often called in here to train together. It's so sad we lost him at such a young age. He'd lot more energy than the rest of us and was such a fit guy."

Jenny had to agree. Andy had not only been a great friend of Steve's, but also a good neighbour for a while, and Steve had sometimes brought him back for supper after their Tuesday night fitness training sessions. Andy was also a doctor in the hospital where Auntie Sue had worked.

Andy continued, "I'm usually here about seven o'clock on Tuesday evenings if I'm not on duty in Accident & Emergency. In two weeks' time I'm going off on a trek to Nepal in the Himalayas as a Medical Officer with the Team. It was great to get this wee volunteering job. I can indulge my love of mountain climbing and do some volunteering work at a small rural clinic at the same time!"

"That's brilliant," said Jenny. "I know a few other folks who've been to Nepal, including one of my brother Ricky's friends, who goes trekking in that part of the world every year."

"It certainly is a great place for trekking," added Andy. "I've already done this a couple of times myself, when I climbed one of the mountain ranges near Pokhara, but this time I'm going to an area in the central region of the country where a small health clinic is based. It's quite a remote location, and one of my other work colleagues is already there on a gap year, helping to run the clinic. He sees lots of TB cases from the area, as well as patients with fractures and spinal injuries. Some of these fracture injuries might have been the result of falling from trees or slipping on the high mountain paths."

Jenny quietly responded, "I'd love to do something like that myself, Andy, but I'm pretty busy at the moment. I don't think I'm fit enough to climb those Himalayan mountains: I'd be breathless walking in the thin air at the high altitudes. I hardly survived ten minutes on the cross-trainer this evening!"

Andy laughed. "I wouldn't worry too much," he continued. "You'd not be alone if you ever fancied visiting at a later date. I've recently been doing some training at the Mourne Mountains in County Down myself, but I don't think I'll get time to do much climbing in Nepal as I'll probably spend most of my time at the clinic. A couple of other guys from the Belfast City Hospital Accident & Emergency Department are also planning to head out with me to do a bit of research about the long-term effects of leprosy that's still prevalent in parts of the country. We're also hoping to bring out some small items of clothing to give to needy patients at the clinic as many of them might have walked for miles to reach any kind of medical help. Do you know of anyone who might be able to donate us some items?"

Carole, who'd been standing nearby and overheard part of the conversation, then joined the chat. "I think you're talking to the right person, Andy. Jenny's recently done some knitting, and she's already made a few gorgeous little knitted kids' sweaters. She's already sent one to Sudan though my niece who did a medical elective there and also sent one to Romania, another to a Syrian refugee family in a large Calais camp, and a further one to Mexico City. I know she finished another one last weekend when she babysat her niece in Helens Bay, and it's now hidden in a bag in my boot. She even showed it to me when we were getting our gym gear out of my car, and it's got a lovely little airplane on the front!"

"Gosh, that sounds great, Jenny," said Andy. "You're certainly keeping yourself busy. I wouldn't mind you knitting me one of those tunics! The Himalayas can be really cold at this time of year and I could put it in my suitcase! However, I'll certainly pass on any smaller ones that you wish to donate."

After a further short chat, Jenny and Carole headed off the female changing room, whilst Andy made for the showers.

About twenty minutes later, they all met up again in the foyer of the Gym. Andy strode over to a nearby water dispenser, filled two small plastic disposable cups with water and handed one each to Jenny and Carole.

"That's very kind of you, Andy," said Jenny, as Andy handed over the cups. "I was ready for that. I think I'll not push myself so much next week. Five minutes on the cross-trainer will be my limit for a while!"

As Andy and Jenny chatted on, Carole left them and went out to her car. A few moments later, she returned with a small plastic bag. She opened it and lifted out Jenny's most recent small sweater, which she'd knitted at Ricky and Lisa's, and handed it to Andy. "That looks super, Jenny," Andy responded with a smile. "Remember, when I'm away in Nepal I wouldn't mind you knitting me a bigger one for our cold winters!"

Jenny and Carole then laughed. "I don't think Jenny has enough wool left to make you a sweater, Andy," said Carole. "You'll just have to wait until you come home. Seriously, we'll all be looking forward to hearing about your time in Nepal, both your mountain trekking and your voluntary work at the clinic."

"Seems a done deal", said Andy. "Jenny can give her hands a rest in the meantime."

A few moments later, Andy gently placed the small sweater back into the plastic bag and put it into his sports bag.

"I'll put this small sweater to good use. I'll make sure it's packed in my luggage with a few other items for the clinic, and my hiking boots will be squashed in, too!" Andy continued.

"Thanks so much, Andy," said Jenny. "I'd love to see the little sweater going to someone who needs it. Maybe if you get a free moment, you'd let Carole or me know how you're surviving. You can send us a quick text or email if there's a wi-fi connection around."

"Will do," said Andy. "I'd better head off now. I'm on duty at eight o'clock in the morning and need to get some sleep. I might see you at the gym next week. If not, I'll look out for you both when I get back from my trip."

Andy then headed off to meet another friend before leaving the gym. Carole and Jenny finished sipping their cups of water, gathered up their gym gear and headed to the car park.

Three weeks later...

Jenny came home after another visit to the gym and muttered, "I think I'll have a nice hot bath with a few drops of lavender scent! Work's been a bit busy these last few days, and my aching feet could do with a bit of a soak, not to mention the aches in my back!" That's exactly what Jenny organised next. After a half hour of gently relaxing under bubbles in the bathtub, Jenny felt refreshed and climbed out of the bath, before heading to the radiator to grab a nice fluffy towel. As she bent down to dry her soggy, wet feet she quietly whispered to herself, "I think that's my mobile phone ringing in the bedroom." There definitely was a small highly pitched ringing noise, so she quickly put on her dressing gown, opened the bathroom door and headed to the bedroom to answer the phone. Just before she pressed the answer button the phone rang off. Jenny then glanced at the screen to read the number of her missed call and saw it was Carole's. She'd also been at the gym that evening. "Wonder why she's phoned?

I only spoke to her about an hour and a half ago," Jenny thought to herself as she dialled 901 and listened to Carole's voicemail. Carole seemed distressed...

"Jenny, I've just heard some terrible news. It's about Andy who's in Nepal right now." Jenny was surprised. She'd seen pictures of Andy on the phone of one of his friends at the gym that evening. He looked well and had been trekking in a very steep part of the Himalayan foothills earlier that afternoon in Ghorahi district, which was in the central belt of the country. Carole continued, "There's been a terrible earthquake and the worst of it seems to be near the district where Andy and his team were climbing today. I got a text from Conan, one of Andy's friends, who mentioned no one's heard from Andy since the earthquake struck. I believe it's one of the worst earthquakes to hit Nepal for decades. I think you'd better switch on the news, Jenny. It'll tell you a lot more details. The whole thing seems quite dreadful..."

Jenny appreciated Carole sending her a voicemail without delay. Before wasting any more time, Jenny switched off her phone and rushed downstairs to put on the TV News channel...

At the bottom of the screen she could see a breaking news summary. A huge earthquake had struck Nepal, measuring 7.8 on the Richter Scale, the worst tremor for nearly a century. At least 4,000 people were confirmed dead, with hundreds more trapped or missing. The worst hit area was in Central Nepal, with whole villages wiped out in less than a minute. Emergency teams were already on the ground, trying to reach bodies trapped since the earth tremor struck. Many of dead and injured seemed to be children.

"Oh no. I pray Andy's alright," Jenny quietly uttered to herself as she stared at the TV. A report then beamed onto the screen from Kathmandu, the capital city. Jenny could see large buildings had fallen to the ground whilst people and animals walked around through clouds of dust. A number of centuries' old buildings, including city temples, seemed to have been reduced to rubble in a matter of seconds despite withstanding former earthquake tremors and shocks. Jenny then heard a reporter saying, "Many are trapped in the capital. Hundreds more are missing in villages near the epicentre of the earthquake, including tourists and a number of mountain climbers."

This was followed by aerial images from a small aircraft flying over a range of shattered rural mountain villages, showing major damage to homes and public buildings. The airborne reporter gently shared harrowing details of the devastation below as the aircraft lowered in altitude. "I can make out people running away from falling buildings and others frantically searching for survivors, even with their bare hands. There's also a number of lifeless bodies lying on the ground." Being a nurse, Jenny could guess what some of the survivors' injuries were likely to be, fractures and wounds caused by broken glass and debris, or crush injuries from falling masonry. She just wished this whole nightmare wasn't happening and that Andy and the rest of his team were safe and dry. There was no way of knowing if any of them were dead or alive at this stage. Like thousands more, she'd just have to wait for what could be good or bad news. Many old and young lives would never be the same again.

Jenny tried to phone Carole back, but there was no reply. She realised there was nothing practical she could do at the moment, so she decided to have an early night. It was actually a warm, early spring evening but cloud cover made the dark seem darker. As Jenny was about to get into bed, she said a prayer for Andy and for all those who were suffering from the earthquake in Nepal. At times like this it was hard to understand why disasters happened, but she knew there'd also be stories of kindness and bravery as rescue attempts got underway.

Jenny lay down and put her head on her pillow at the top of the bed. "I feel like I'm suffocating," she thought to herself, as she felt the weight of her duvet over her body and images from Nepal swirled around in her head. "It must be awful to be trapped under a fallen building." She also couldn't help thinking that some mountain climbers like Andy could even be trapped under an avalanche of fallen rocks at the top of the higher mountains. "I really hope Andy is safe." Jenny couldn't help wondering if Andy's small clinic was still standing, as it seemed to be in an area near the earthquake epicentre. If he'd survived, he'd be a tremendous help with giving assistance and sharing his medical skills. "At least he's an experienced doctor, he's fit, and he's also got some useful "gifts" to share, even if one of them is only a small woollen sweater," Jenny whispered as she drifted off to sleep. A short while later she started to dream about a small child near a broken building, shocked and shivering with cold and waiting for help to come...

CHAPTER THIRTEEN

PARBATI'S STORY (NEPAL)

Little Parbati lay in darkness, crushed below the rubble. Her right leg was trapped under a broken door frame and she could barely breathe in the small confined space. It was hard to believe that only a few hours ago she'd arrived at the town of Nepalganj, in central Nepal, with her grandmother to buy candles and soap at the bazaar.

"Grandmother Laxhmi. Where are you? I can't see you," Parbati called out as soft tears slowly trickled down her cheeks and her right leg kept throbbed with pain. "I can hardly breathe and there's lots of dust in my mouth," she mumbled. "I wish I could turn my head, but I can't, and a huge piece of concrete is pressing down on top of my chest." Parbati could hear the voices of children and adults close by, but none of them sounded like her grandmother Laxhmi.

Parbati had lost track of time. She could vaguely remember getting up before sunrise to walk to Nepalganj with Laxhmi along two steep Himalayan mountain paths, slipping and sliding for most of the way, then stopping at a teashop near the bazaar. Laxhmi had just sat down at a small table when there was a huge rumbling sound that seemed to come straight out of the earth and the whole building had started to shake. Parbati then remembered a huge crack appearing on the wall in front of her before a tingling sensation started in her legs, then her knees gave way and she fell to the ground. This must have been the big earthquake that many people had been talking about.

"I wish I'd never come to the bazaar," thought Parbati as she clenched her teeth in pain. "I could have stayed at home and helped mother with preparing the lentil dahl for supper." Now she had to wait for rescue with memories of the morning before the earthquake struck – small boys pulling carts, rickshaw drivers weaving in and out of pedestrians, cows chewing fodder as they walked on the road, cars honking their horns and women carrying baskets of corn and fruit to sell at the Nepalganj bazaar.

Parbati tried to move her right leg but it was still firmly trapped. "How am I going to walk with grandmother Laxhmi for four hours to and from the village well each day to collect water for drinking, cooking and washing if my leg doesn't work?" she muttered, though there seemed no one close enough to hear. "I'll not to be able to carry a basket of firewood on my back on the steep mountain trails anymore." Lots of Nepali women had strong muscles in their backs and legs, as they had to walk each day in the hot sun carrying heavy filled baskets. Laxhmi's lined face and shrunken body were testament that she'd done this herself for over forty years since she was a little girl, even younger than Parbati was now. The collected firewood was often used for lighting fires or to burn as fuel, particularly in the cooler months after the monsoon rains. "I've lost my right flip flop," Parbati whispered as she gave a low moan. "And I think my sari is ripped and covered in mud." Like most of the women and girls in her village, a sari was the main garment that females wore each day along with sandals for walking. She also wore her glossy black hair in a plait tied with a red ribbon at the back of her head. Many of her mother's friends also wore colourful bangles on their wrists and ankles, often received as part of a dowry when they got married.

Parbati bit her lip and tried to gently control her breath as she thought a bit more about her normal village life in the mountains...

She liked living with her mother Uzeli, her father Himal, her younger brothers Puran and Dipak, and of course grandmother Lahxmi. Laxhmi had lived in the village since she'd got married, just like many other women from rural areas of Nepal, and Uzeli was her only daughter. Her other children had all been boys, but only two had survived; the rest died as small babies shortly after birth. Parbati knew she was extra special to Laxhmi, as not only was she the oldest grandchild, she was also always keen to learn new things and this made her feel positive as she lay in the dark.

A few moments later a little panic feeling started as Parbati thought about her father. "I wish you didn't have to go away to India last week to get a job," she quietly sobbed. Himal often had to leave home to search for work in Kathmandu, the capital city of Nepal, or in India or Tibet. A few days ago, he'd gone to Mumbai to do a labouring job, but sometimes he stayed in the village to help gather maize at harvest time, which didn't pay very much. As Parbati's breath got shallower, she tried to imagine she was back at home...

She liked helping Uzeli with feeding the goats, sweeping the floors and sifting the rice husks before Uzeli cooked the rice with dhal bhat (lentil curry) in the evenings over a charcoal fire for the main family meal. She didn't mind keeping a watchful eye on Puran and Dipak when Uzeli was busy. Parbati wished she could go to the village school with Puran, who started to attend in the afternoons after his seventh birthday. Dipak was only two and usually crawled about the house or along the outdoor path, but Uzeli often worried he'd get bitten by a snake.

Parbati also wanted to go to school, but there was no extra money or opportunity for a girl like her to get there. She was nearly twelve, and in a few years' time she'd probably be married off to a distant cousin or a local man in the village. Parbati started to feel very drowsy and began to drift into sleep when she suddenly heard voices very close by. "Over here. I think there's a young girl under this pile of rubble." Parbati felt a large piece of concrete starting to move above her head and less pressure on her right leg.

"That hurts," she blurted out as a light beamed into her eyes. A Nepali man's voice quietly told her to "stay calm," before she felt a strong tugging feeling on her legs. Several hands seemed to pull her from the rubble and dragged her into the street outside, well away from the collapsed building. As Parbati gazed around she couldn't help blinking in the strong sunshine: everything looked so different from what she'd seen that morning. Electric cables were strewn across the street, nearby temples had lost their roofs, cars were crushed like flattened cans, and piles of debris lay everywhere. Several injured and dead bodies lay on the ground.

Parbati couldn't help bursting into tears as she uttered, "I want to go home. I need to find my grandmother Laxhmi and my right leg's very sore." As Parbati sobbed she watched several policemen, some soldiers and other workers with Red Crosses on their T shirts lifting other people from the rubble and placing them onto stretchers. Some of the ones with Red Crosses had little necklaces around their necks which they were pressing onto peoples' chests. Parbati later found out that these were called stethoscopes to monitor heartbeats.

A few moments later Parbati was lifted into the air and onto a stretcher herself. The next thing she knew was waking up in a large building at the far end of the town which hadn't been damaged in the earthquake...

Parbati couldn't believe there were so many people with broken bones and nasty cuts as she looked around the room. "They must have been trapped like me or hit by falling debris," Parbati thought, as a lady who looked like a nurse walked over to her side.

"What's your name?" the nurse asked.

"Parbati," the little girl replied, now shivering with post-traumatic shock.

"That's a nice name," said the nurse. "I'm going to clean up the nasty wound in your right leg. I'll try to be a quick as I can." Just then, the other nurse, who had a pale face, came over with a small basin in her hand.

"You're a very brave girl," the nurse with the basin said. "I'm also going to help you get nice and comfortable after the awful day you've had."

As the two nurses gently washed the dust and blood from Parbati's leg, the water stung a lot, but Parbati knew it would help to heal and cleanse her leg. Parbati clenched her hands and teeth as one of the nurses carefully removed her small rubber flip-flop sandals and peeled her damp cotton sari off her injured limb. She then opened a bandage and carefully wound it around Parbati's right leg.

As she worked, Parbati mumbled, "My leg feels sore and prickly," as she continued to shake from shock.

Soon the now faint light from outside started to fade, as the two nurses left Parbati to attend some other newly arrived patients on stretchers. Parbati looked down and saw her main body was still covered in dust. "I wish I could see grandmother Laxhmi," Parbati softly mumbled, as she started to feel drowsy again. "I hope she isn't hurt like me." Parbati also wished someone would give her a little cardigan or sweater as she was now starting to feel cold.

In no time, Parbati drifted off to sleep again. When she woke up, she didn't know she'd slept for nearly three days…

Parbati felt startled and confused before she recognised her mother's face. Tears were rolling down Uzeli's face as she spoke. "Parbati, we've been looking for you for almost four days. Your father came back from India when he heard about the earthquake and helped in the search for you. I'm so glad we found you alive."

Parbati was thrilled to see her mother, then asked, "Where's grandmother Laxhmi?"

Uzeli looked sad as she answered. "Grandma was hurt in the earthquake. Her hand was badly damaged and she's in a large hospital in Kathmandu, but she's going to recover. She's been worried about you, too." Parbati was glad to know grandmother Laxhmi had survived.

"When can we go home?" Parbati then asked.

Uzeli looked troubled. "It's going to be some time, Parbati," she replied. "The road to our village was damaged, and nearly all the houses have lost their roofs. Even the bridge over the river collapsed. Many cows and goats have been killed and most of the village crops have been destroyed. But some kind people came to visit us yesterday and gave us blankets, bread and fruit." Uzeli took a small guava from the basket she was carrying and gave it to Parbati. She continued, "We've also been given some tools to start vegetable gardens and emergency food rations. The visitors promised they'll come back soon to build new latrines and repair the bridge over the river." Parbati knew that some of these people may have come from other lands after the earthquake.

As Parbati took a bite of the guava fruit, a man with a pale face who looked like a doctor walked over to her side. He gently asked, "Could I remove the bandage on your right leg and check the wound underneath?" Parbati nodded her head as he gently carried out his task. "You've been a very good patient, Parbati, and your leg is healing well. I know you were asleep for a long time, but this has given your body time to heal. Dr Singh, a surgeon, operated on the bones and ligaments in your foot, and you're going to be OK. You should soon be able to walk with a stick." Parbati felt a bit anxious when she heard that. She needed two strong legs to climb up and down the steep mountain paths with a heavy basket on her back, supported by a strap from her forehead.

Uzeli gently comforted her. "Don't worry, Parbati," she said. "You'll soon be fit and strong again. When grandmother comes back from Kathmandu, she'll look after Puran and Dipak while you help me start a small vegetable garden. Puran might even get back to school."

Parbati knew some of her village neighbours sent their children away to places like Thailand or India to work instead of going to school, and sometimes they didn't come back. She certainly didn't like that. She hoped she'd someday learn to read and write herself so she could teach others in her village.

A few moments later, the doctor stooped down before lifting a small red sweater from a bag on the floor. "This is a little gift for you, Parbati. It was made by a lady who lives in the country I come from, and she wanted me to give it to someone who'd be able to wear it every day. I think you'll find it useful during the chilly nights after the monsoon. You can even wear it now." The doctor handed the knitted sweater to Uzeli, who then placed it over Parbati's head. As Parbati pushed her head through the hole in the neckline she immediately felt the soft wool rubbing against her arms and also loved the little aeroplane motif on the front. She knew real aeroplanes flew high in the sky, sometimes over her village. Right now, she didn't need to shiver in the cold or wonder if she'd get a new sari to replace her damaged one. Some kind person must have been knitting...

The doctor spoke again, just before he had to leave to attend another patient, "Parbati, my name's Andy and I come from a place called Belfast in Northern Ireland, but I'm staying here in Nepalganj for another short while. I think you're a real survivor and I'm going to tell my family and friends about you when I go home. One of my friends called Jenny made your little sweater. She'll be so proud to hear about you and to know how brave you've been. I'll be able to let her know that that you're getting stronger every day. Maybe sometime soon I'll come back to Nepal."

As Andy walked away, Uzeli gently helped Parbati to stand on her feet. Soon she'd be back in her village, climbing up and down the mountains with grandmother Laxhmi, wearing her new red sweater over her sari. She wanted all her neighbours, her family, and of course herself, to get back to normal again... without a stick.

CHAPTER FOURTEEN

JENNY AT EBOLA TALK

Jenny puffed and panted as she reached the top of the stairs on the third floor of the Health Centre, then glanced at her watch. "Gosh. I didn't realise it was so late," she muttered. "I must have been talking to Carole longer than I thought on the phone this morning." Jenny had been so glad to hear Andy had survived the Nepal earthquake and was spending a bit more time helping survivors before his came home that she hadn't realised the time. "I'd better get a move on," Jenny mumbled. Her training was due to start in five minutes. It was a seminar about the recent Ebola crisis on the west coast of Africa. Although it was highly unlikely that the virus would reach the UK, there were still a number of ways it could cross continents, and all the district nurses in Belfast were advised to attend. Jenny knew that a number of local people regularly travelled to Africa on business or for a holiday and could be easily be infected. A young couple from her own church had recently gone to Senegal for six months to help with literature translation work. She hoped they'd be okay.

Jenny headed straight for Room 4 opposite the stairs. As she entered the room, she noticed most seats were filled, so she headed to a row at the back and sat down. She just made it on time, as the first speaker was just starting her presentation, supported by slides on a PowerPoint screen behind.

"The recent Ebola virus seemed to start around Sierra Leone, but has now crossed borders into Liberia, Guinea Bissau and Nigeria. Hundreds are currently ill, and the death toll is rising. Most hospitals or clinics in these countries do not have adequate resources for patient treatment or decontamination sites. There is a high risk of cross infection on public transport as many patients travel by bus or taxi from bush villages to access treatment sites. If they reach their destinations, most of them have to sleep on makeshift beds or on mats outside, as they couldn't be admitted to the usual medical wards. Many leave it too late to arrive for medical help and often relatives of the deceased insist that bodies are to be returned to the home village for burial." Jenny knew this would pose a major risk for spreading infection, especially in a hot climate, and diseased bodies would need to be buried quickly or even cremated. The speaker continued, "Some tribal groups believe the souls of their departed relatives will not rest in peace unless they are buried in their own home village."

One of Jenny's colleagues called Sandra had recently returned from West Africa and already told her this herself. She'd also mentioned she'd had to pass through very tight security at the airports in Sierra Leone and at Heathrow on her return, and subsequently had to go into quarantine for five days in case she showed signs of Ebola.

The speaker then mentioned a case that had been on the UK News, "A nurse from Scotland recently contacted the disease and is still being treated in an isolation ward in Edinburgh, fighting for her life. She is to be trialled as a guinea pig for a new Ebola treatment, and if it works, it could potentially be a cure for thousands of others in affected parts of the world."

This was most encouraging information before further statistics and figures were put up on the screen. A short time later, this first talk came to an end, followed by a short twenty-minute break. Jenny was glad to get up from her seat to stretch her limbs, then decided to head off to the Health Centre café for a cup of tea.

Jenny paid for her hot drink, plus a small scone, then headed for an empty table near the door, where she could leave quickly for a toilet stop before the next talk, when she spotted Sandra, her friend who'd recently returned from Africa. She hadn't realised Sandra was also at the seminar and must have been sitting near the front of the room. Sandra waved as Jenny walked over to join her.

"Hi, Sandra," Jenny said. "I've just been at one of the Ebola talks. I found it interesting but also very sad, and I know you were recently in the thick of it yourself, treating patients with this disease."

"I certainly was, Jenny," Sandra responded. "Hundreds of people arrived every day for treatment and I had to wear a special body isolation suit. It was heart breaking to see many small children and older people succumbing to the disease. My Team aimed to give everyone the appropriate medication and emergency treatment, and basic diet supplements to halt the disease from spreading. Some of the children at the decontamination centre had hardly any clothes or possessions."

"Are you planning to go back to Sierra Leone?" Jenny asked.

Sandra replied, "I'm returning next month if I get clearance from occupational health. I'm still working for one of the GP's here, but he's happy to let me go off again on another short contract if he can find another locum nurse. I've had all the required vaccinations, so I'm in a good position to disappear again. I'm planning to bring some small garments to Sierra Leone with me, such as little T shirts or sweaters. The small children I'll be treating, especially the orphaned kids, could really make use of them. I must try to find some folk who could supply these."

Jenny then started to smile. "Maybe I could start your collection, Sandra. I've a small knitted tunic in my handbag and would be happy to donate it to you. I knitted it a few days ago when I'd a weekend off. Why don't we find a seat and I can tell you more?"

Jenny then lifted her tray with her purchased mug of tea and scone and headed for one of the canteen tables. Sandra followed behind with a cup of decaf coffee. They both sat down as Jenny chatted about finding her Auntie Sue's old knitting bag and pattern, and how her knitting skills had since been resurrected! "You'll not believe it, Sandra, but I've already knitted five sweaters that have travelled overseas. My Auntie Sue used to bring little sweaters with her on her nursing trips, and I think I want to continue what she started!" Sandra was delighted to hear all this. Jenny then reached into her handbag and lifted out her latest small sweater before handing it to Sandra. It had a small boat motif on the front which she'd only sewn on the previous evening.

"Many thanks, Jenny," said Sandra. "I'll take this with me to Africa, and some small child will be glad of it. So many little ones have lost nearly everything because of Ebola, and not just their health. A small sweater could really make the difference between life and death."

Sandra then briefly told Jenny more details about where she'd be based this time, a large school called Hope Academy, just outside Freetown, the capital city. Her main job would be screening school pupils for signs of Ebola, but she might also get to treat patients in some of the rural emergency decontamination centres.

Jenny listened, then gently smiled before she spoke. "You're not going to believe this, Sandra. I just received an email at the weekend from Carley, the daughter of a lady called Pearl who I met at a recent knitting workshop, and she's a teacher in that very place. I understand a number of the pupils in Hope Academy have already caught Ebola, and all the staff have been advised to wear protective garments."

"It's a small world! Fancy you having a connection with the school where I'm to be based," said Sandra. "On a more serious note, I've received similar facts to yours. As I'm going to be one of the nurses who's to carry out the next phase of the screening programme, I'll have to adhere to strict infection control guidelines myself, including wearing a body suit if I need to. A number of the schools in Sierra Leone, Guinea Bissau, Liberia and Senegal will have to follow the same procedures."

Jenny was pleased Sandra would be a connection from home for Pearl's daughter, and added, "No doubt you and Carley both will have lots to tell when you return, as you're both going to be on the frontline relief efforts."

As the two nurses finished their hot drinks, Sandra asked Jenny a question: "Would you ever think of going on a short trip overseas yourself? I don't necessarily mean to an Ebola-infected place, but maybe another location where you could share your nursing skills?"

Jenny hesitated for a moment. "Do you know, Sandra?" she replied. "I've hadn't really thought of that. I guess I've been so focused on sorting Steve's estate and clearing away his stuff that I haven't considered a lot beyond my immediate world for a while. Having said that, finding and knitting Auntie Sue's old sweater knitting pattern has really challenged me, and I can't stop thinking about the small children overseas who've already received the small garments I made. Maybe sometime I could head off myself."

"Well, Jenny," said Sandra. "I'll give you advice if you ever need it, but I'd better run on now. I've to assist at a GP surgery this morning, as some of the staff are on Annual Leave, so I'll not head back to the seminar until after lunch."

Sandra then went off to treat her patients as Jenny stacked their used cups onto a tray and carried it to the stacking trolley beside the door, before a quick trip to the ladies' toilet. "Better be quick," Jenny thought. "I've only five minutes before the next lecture starts. It'll make me appreciate what Pearl and Sandra need to cope with and also how to stop the virus coming here."

Five minutes later, Jenny returned to the lecture.

CHAPTER FIFTEEN

NOUHOU'S STORY (SIERRA LEONE)

A month later, Jenny received an email from Sandra, based at Hope Academy in Sierra Leone. Another of Jenny's small sweaters had cheered up a young child with a story to tell...

Nouhou lived in a small concrete bungalow in a township outside Freetown, situated not too far from his school. One morning he woke early, even before the cockerel crowed outside, and felt a bit feverish.

"My head aches and I've a sore throat," he whispered, as he slowly dragged himself up from his sleeping mattress on the floor. "I don't like the look of those blotchy bruises on my skin," he added as he stared at his forearms and the back of his hands. He was sure the blotches weren't there the day before. "I really don't want to get sick," Nouhou mumbled under his breath. "I need to keep well so I help grandmother harvest her groundnuts."

Sadly, some of Nouhou's school friends had caught something nasty and hadn't been around for a few weeks, and Nouhou hoped whatever they had they didn't reach him! Nouhou's grandfather Kamara, a former village chief, had caught the AIDS virus a few years before, and lots of neighbours were scared to visit him when he was sick. Nouhou certainly didn't want that to happen to him.

After Nouhou slowly stood up, he staggered outside to the latrine before walking over to the plastic bucket that hung from one of the branches of the large banyan tree and had a quick shower. As he washed his face and hands, he could hear Solomon, his seven year old brother, taking to his mum, Favour, inside the house.

"Get Nouhou to lift the eggs from the chickens before you go to school, and remember to buy some bananas at the market on your way home." Nouhou didn't hear the rest of the conversation as he slowly shuffled back into the house to put on his school uniform which was a white shirt, black trousers, a blue tie and a dark blue sweater, the same as Solomon had.

"I wish I'd a schoolbag, but there's isn't enough money to buy one," Nouhou thought as he heard his mother calling.

"Nouhou," she shouted. "Your injura is cooked and you need to come and eat it now or you'll be late for school."

Nouhou called out a weak reply. "I'm coming."

A few minutes later, as Nouhou slowly forced himself to eat his bowl of injura and tried to drink some goat's milk from an old gourd, he announced, "I'm not feeling hungry. In fact, I feel quite sick." His appetite had simply disappeared. After attempting breakfast, he then walked outside to the chickens and gathered six eggs, putting them into a small woven basket. He then carried them into the house and gave them to Favour, who was peeling sweet potatoes for a meal in the evening.

"Thanks, Nouhou," Favour said. "I'm worried you haven't eaten much breakfast. Maybe you've a fever coming on. As you're walking to school please stay on the main paths and get Solomon to come back with you if you need to come home early."

Nouhou agreed as he collected his only notebook and pencil and joined Solomon at the door to make tracks for school.

As Nouhou and Solomon walked along one of the main roads in the township, they couldn't believe the number of bicycles, trucks and cars passing by. "Look where you're going, we could easily get knocked down because some of these drivers are going very fast," Nouhou warned his younger brother as several drivers honked their horns and tried to overtake them.

"At least the rains haven't come yet and made the roads all slippery," Solomon responded. Nouhou nodded in agreement, as he knew cars often got stuck in the mud at that time of the year.

Nouhou and Solomon soon reached the path at the edge of the largest river that ran through the township. "Please hold onto me," Solomon called out as they reached the path, "I'm scared a crocodile is going to jump out of the water." The boys were always a bit scared on this path, as one of Favour's friends had been killed by a crocodile when she washed clothes in the river a few years before.

A few minutes later, the boys breathed a sigh of relief when they safely reached the end of this path. "At least we haven't far to go now," said Nouhou to encourage Solomon. "There's only a few alleyways before we see our school." Nouhou started to feel quite queasy when he saw several pot-bellied pigs munching their way through piles of rotting garbage and nearly stumbled into some puddles as he walked behind Solomon, trying not to trip on the old tin cans and floating bottles that lay around. Eventually the walls of Faith Academy loomed up ahead. "Meet me after school so we can walk home together," Nouhou said, as the boys reached the large wooden doors at the front of the school building. "Class four might not get out as early as Class two today, but you can wait for me here." Solomon nodded his head as he skipped off to his class while Nouhou made his way to Class four.

When Nouhou reached his classroom, his friends Abdul and Omar were already seated at a long communal desk. It was good to have them as buddies as Abdul was good at maths and Omar was good at spellings. As Nouhou sat down between his friends, Mr Kamara, the Class Four teacher, walked into the room and addressed the class. "Good morning, pupils," he said.

All the pupils stood up and replied, "Good Morning, sir."

Everyone then sat down before Mr Kamara stood at the front and announced, "Lessons will end earlier today, as there's going to be a health inspection for the whole school."

Most of the class pupils looked around at each other in shock but some were glad as they'd worms or head lice and wanted to see a doctor or nurse. A few were also recovering from a recent bout of measles.

After that the morning seemed to pass quickly. Nouhou didn't feel himself at all but practiced copying the spellings that Mr Kamara had written on the board and also attempted some arithmetic exercises with a bit of help from Abdul!

"I don't think my writing's too good today," Nouhou said to Omar as he looked at his spidery writing on the page. "My hand's a bit shaky." Omar had to agree as Nouhou was usually a neat writer and always took great care of his notebook. He knew Nouhou even kept it in cardboard box beside his rolled up sleeping mattress.

Later, when there was a short midday break for lunch, Nouhou went outside to use the only school latrine. As he waited, he started to sniff and cough and still didn't feel awfully well. "I'm too hot and my belly hurts," he mumbled to himself as he reached the front of the long queue. When he eventually used the latrine, diarrhoea struck, so things weren't looking good.

Nouhou ate a bit of mango and drank some water from an old flask before returning to his classroom for the afternoon lessons. A pleasant teacher called Miss Gray arrived to teach an English class.

"I think she's from Northern Ireland, but I'm not sure where that is," Omar whispered as he helped Nouhou sharpen his pencil before writing in his notebook. "Someone told me her name is Carley, but I don't think we should call her that at school. Teachers should always be shown respect." Nouhou had to agree.

Miss Gray proceeded to start telling a short story when the head teacher walked into the room. He went straight over to Miss Gray and quietly shared some information. Miss Gray appeared to nod, gave a slight cough then made an announcement to the class. "Please put away your pencils and jotters and line up at the door. All of you are to proceed to the school assembly hall for your health inspection."

Nouhou, Omer and Abdul then followed the rest of the class down a long corridor to the assembly hall where two long queues of pupils were already waiting to be seen. After what seemed like ages, Omar and Abdul were directed to a queue at one side of the room whilst Nouhou was asked to wait at the front of the other one. A few moments later, his name was called for inspection.

A nurse with golden coloured hair and the same colour skin as Miss Gray's stood up from her desk. She instructed Nouhou to "stick out his tongue," before swabbing it with a tiny sponge, then said, "I'm going to comb your hair to check for any lice," whilst she lifted a small comb from the desk in front of her and gently pulled it through his hair. Then she made another request. "Please raise your left arm so I can check your temperature with this small thermometer." Nouhou did as he was told but started to feel dizzy as he'd been standing quite a long time at that stage. The nurse then listened to his heartbeat with a stethoscope and checked his eyes for infection.

Suddenly, she looked a bit shocked and said, "Please step aside." Before anything else was mentioned, Nouhou was quickly ushered from the assembly hall into a small room at the rear of the building, without getting the chance to alert Abdul and Omar, who still waited for their own inspections. As Nouhou looked around the small room he spotted several other pupils, including two from Solomon's class.

A few moments later, a large white van pulled up outside, an outer door was opened, and four people entered the room. They wore white body suits from head to toe, including plastic visors on their faces and gloves on their hands. Nouhou pondered to himself, "They must be very hot, it's over thirty degrees outside."

Nouhou then started to feel frightened as one of people in a white suit said, "You're all going to be taken from school today to a special clinic to get some treatment." Before any of the pupils could object, they were ushered outside and into the waiting white van. When the last child got on board, the rear van door was closed and the vehicle quickly drove away from the school. Nouhou and the other kids hadn't a clue where they were going or what was happening and some of the children started to cry. All of them weren't feeling well and most looked flushed and feverish, which only made things even worse. As Nouhou looked out the window, he suddenly spotted a large white tent in the distance. "I think we must be near the big district hospital," he thought as he recognised a few signs on the road. In no time, the van was driven up a long path and stopped in front of the large white tent. Another person in a full body suit walked out of the tent and came over to the doorway of the van, with the following order, "Please step out as quickly as you can and follow me." As Nouhou and the other children did as they told, it was hard not to stare at the loads of people who were also arriving in tax-is or buses, all of them looking very weak.

The Hope Academy pupils were directed to one of the corners of the tent and asked to sit on plastic chairs. A short time later, the nurse whom Nouhou recognised as the one who'd completed his health inspection, arrived at the tent in a body suit herself. She seemed to know a lot of the other workers.

"I'm Sandra," she explained to Nouhou and the other pupils from the school. "You're all here because your school health inspection identified a dangerous virus and you need some special help." Sandra then opened a white plastic bag and pulled out what looked like special pyjamas for each child. "Please remove your outer clothes before you put these on," she ordered. Nouhou was a bit upset as he didn't want to lose his nice white shirt and blue jumper. Following Sandra's instructions, the Hope Academy pupils were then led to another section of the tent where a number of other children had already arrived, all with red rimmed eyes and small raised rashes on their arms. Nouhou realised he must have caught the nasty virus that was going around his village, as he'd also got some problems like them. As each child was directed to sit down on a mat on the floor, another nurse arrived and gave further information. "Don't be worrying," she said. "You're not going to be here for long. You're all going to get some treatment to make you feel better so you can safely return home to your families. Your Head Teachers are going to contact your parents or guardians to let them know you're here."

One of the younger children sobbed and said, "I want to go home now."

The nurse replied, "You're not very well, but you'll be home very soon if you take your medicine and stay indoors." As she spoke, Nouhou noticed some people being carried out of the tent in stretchers who didn't move at all. Perhaps they'd arrived too late or didn't take their medicine in time.

Two weeks later...

The nurse called Sandra arrived at the tent. She walked over to Nouhou and the other Hope Academy pupils to give them some good news. "You're all doing very well and should be recovered very soon. The fortified porridge you've been eating has helped to fight the Ebola and you'll be able to return to your villages and back to school. You'll also not have to wear your special pyjamas anymore. In fact, I've some special presents for each of you, a new garment to take home as some of your other clothes had to be destroyed." Sandra then opened a large cloth bag and lifted out a range of knitted cardigans and sweaters. She handed Nouhou a bright red sweater with a small boat on the front.

"That's cool," he exclaimed, as it was even nicer than the school jumper he'd had before, and it really cheered him up. He'd be able to show it to Solomon and his parents when he got home. In the meantime, he was so glad he'd started to feel better and really hoped none of school friends or relatives got ill. However, he might never have met a special nurse like Sandra if he hadn't had his health inspection. The person who knitted his red sweater had to be special too...

CHAPTER SIXTEEN

MEETING THE NEW GP

"I'd better have an early night as I'm on the early shift in the morning!" Jenny remembered as she went up to the attic to collect the last of Steve's clothes which she planned to leave in a Lisburn Road charity shop. As she rummaged about, Jenny found the large plastic cover from her Ikea mattress and an old striped bedroom rug from the spare room where Steve played his guitar on his free days off. Jenny wrapped the old rug and Steve's clothes inside the plastic cover, ready for taking to the charity shop. As she climbed down the attic staircase, Jenny glanced into the back bedroom and spotted Auntie Sue's red knitting bag. "Flip! I'd forgotten my bag was in there. 'Must have abandoned it when I answered the phone after coming back from the knitting workshop. That was a great night!" Two leftover balls of red wool and Auntie Sue's sweater pattern were still in the bag. As Jenny walked into the bedroom to retrieve them, she remembered she'd have some free time the next evening and could start another small sweater. There was also one leftover small motif of Pearl's that wasn't used, a little fish, and it could be sewn onto the front.

Jenny stayed up for a short while longer. After ironing her nursing uniforms for the week ahead and reading a couple of chapters of a book she'd borrowed from the local library the week before, she yawned and muttered, "I've had enough. I'm heading for bed!" She knew she had to be at the Health Centre for eight AM in the morning to collect her new patient referrals.

As Jenny crossed the landing after going into the bathroom to clean her teeth, she heard a sudden howling noise outside, and the lights began to flicker. "Oh no! I hope there's no power cuts," Jenny whispered to herself, although she knew the weather forecast had predicted a storm during the night with possible structural damage in some exposed places. "I'd better head down to the kitchen for a wee torch just in case." After going downstairs and finding a torch she returned upstairs. She was glad she was safely at home, and not stuck in some remote area or in a place with extreme weather conditions.

A few minutes later, Jenny switched off her bedroom light as she listened to the heavy bursts of rain and howling wind outside. "Time for sleep," she thought.

Morning soon arrived. "Oh no!" Jenny exclaimed." I must have forgotten to switch my alarm clock on after listening to that storm last night." At least it was a Saturday morning and the traffic should be lighter for getting to work.

After a quick bowl of microwaved porridge and literally pulling on her uniform, Jenny left the house in a hurry and drove off to the Health Centre as a sudden hailstorm came down near the traffic lights at the Finaghy Road junction. "I can hardly see where I'm going," Jenny muttered as she tried to make out the newly built apartments and Spar garage on the city bound side of the road.

After struggling through another heavy shower, she eventually reached the Health Centre car park, where it didn't take long to spot damage from the night before. Several tall trees had been uprooted and a number of plants had also been tossed from the large flower bed outside the building's front entrance.

"Oops! I nearly slipped," Jenny exclaimed as she almost fell into a large puddle outside the main reception door. As she walked towards the district nursing office, Jenny hoped she wouldn't have too many patient referrals that day due to the flooded roads. Usually she loved her job, but sometimes she found it hard to cope with her ongoing grief. It was also difficult giving away Steve's old items, but Jenny had decided not to part with Steve's firefighter helmet or his medals. They were a tangible link from his past and a reminder of his great bravery. She really hoped that one day she'd meet someone who could fill her in with more details about what actually happened on the night Steve died.

Jenny suddenly heard a small beep and realised it was her phone. A new email message showed up on the screen. It read,

"Greetings from Sierra Leone. Still working in Hope Academy. Ebola virus is weakening. No new outbreaks near Freetown last week. Will fill you in with lots more details when I come home next month."

Jenny knew this message was from Sandra and was pleased to hear she seemed alright. It was brave of her to go to a place with a high risk of catching serious illness and really looked forward to hearing more about her Sierra Leone experiences when she returned. This prompted another thought in Jenny's head. Perhaps she should think about going on a short overseas project herself, a bit like Auntie Sue used to do, as Sandra suggested. "Must keep my eyes open for the volunteering adverts on the staff noticeboard," Jenny agreed as she headed to the underground equipment store.

Jenny collected a range of dressings and syringes for later in the day and was packing them into her nursing bag when she noticed one of the new GP's, Dr Tan, standing at the doorway. Jenny knew he'd recently arrived from the Philippines to do some medical research at Queens University and was planning to return home to set up a clinic for people with limited financial means. Just now he'd a worried look on his face and was talking on his mobile phone, speaking a native Filipino language and sounding quite distressed. Whatever he was discussing was obviously important.

Jenny hadn't time to speak to him. Her first patient was due for an early morning diabetic insulin injection at 8.30am and she couldn't keep him waiting. At least he didn't live too far away. Plenty of other visits were lined up for the rest of the morning.

Before she knew it, three o'clock arrived. As Jenny turned off the Ormeau Road and into the grounds of Sunnyside Residential Home to meet her next patient, Mrs Clarke, small daffodils lined each side of the driveway and were waving in the breeze. The weather still felt chilly and damp, so Jenny had a thick jacket on over her nursing uniform. Hopefully the warmer weather was coming!

Jenny soon found Mrs Clarke in the dayroom, as it was hard to miss her blue rinsed hair and distinctive giggle! Jenny had already been treating the troublesome ulcers on her legs but now they were almost gone. "I'll put a fresh dressing on each leg and come back to see you next week," Jenny said to Mrs Clarke. "These will keep your skin clean and help your sores to heal." As Jenny put small fresh dressings on Mrs Clarke's ulcers, she was pleased to see her patient back to using a stick after her recent fall.

As Jenny then left Mrs Clarke to write up her nursing notes in the staff office, she spotted a small walled garden at the back of the building. "I wouldn't mind working in a place like this," Jenny couldn't help thinking as two other nurses appeared. Jenny had already met one of them, called Karen, in the care home before. The other nurse introduced herself as Meula and mentioned she came from the Philippines. Jenny thought Meula spoke fluent English in a beautiful tone, but noticed she looked a little tearful. Hopefully, it wasn't about work.

Karen then spoke. "Jenny, please excuse Meula. She's just received some very bad news. There was a violent typhoon in the Philippines last night with the eye of the storm hitting the eastern side of the islands, where her relatives live. She's been frantically trying to make contact with them, but all telephone and email connections seem to be down. She asked her brother who lives here to phone but he's also had difficulty getting a response. I think you might have already met Meula's brother Shu, who's working as a GP at your Health Centre."

It didn't take long for Jenny to work out that Shu was Dr Tan and she responded, "Of course! I do know Dr Tan. In fact, I spotted him talking on his mobile phone earlier this morning and thought he looked very anxious. Now when I think about it, the Philippines typhoon was mentioned on the twelve o'clock news when I'd my car radio on, but I never connected that with Dr Tan."

Meula then spoke, "My brother's hoping to return to the Philippines in the next few days if he can organise the tickets. He's planning to bring extra baggage including basic medical supplies, blankets and small children's clothes. I promised I'd make out some flyers to request further donations of goods."

Karen then stepped forward to say, "Most of our residents' families would be only too happy to help. In fact, some of our ladies might even knit small cardigans or hats." On hearing this, Jenny knew she'd like to contribute in some way herself.

As Meula and Karen suddenly had to leave the office to attend to a resident's needs, Jenny wrote up Mrs Clarke's case notes, then put on her outdoor jacket and headed back to the car. She knew she'd be back at Sunnyside House the following week.

Jenny decided to return to the Health Centre, as she'd seen all her allocated patients for that day. As she joined a queue of cars over the Albert Bridge near the large train station, there seemed to be a problem ahead. The sound of an approaching fire engine got nearer as the traffic started to move. Jenny managed to spot the collision of two cars at the end of the Bridge. One vehicle lay on its side and the other had a badly damaged grille, broken windscreen and smashed front headlights. Within seconds a fire engine pulled up and two firefighters leapt straight to the vehicle on its side, skilfully freeing a young woman who'd been trapped inside.

Jenny wondered if she should assist, but the sight of an approaching ambulance from the other side of the Bridge meant the young woman would get any emergency treatment required. Jenny couldn't help experiencing a tight feeling in her stomach. Watching this scene of frontline workers in action reminded her of how much she missed Steve. She then said a small inward prayer for the two accident victims as she slowly drove on to her office in the Saturday afternoon traffic.

Later that evening, Jenny decided to do a bit more knitting, as Sandra's email from Sierra Leone reminded her that a small sweater could be a blessing or even a life-saver for a young survivor. Jenny climbed upstairs to retrieve Auntie Sue's red knitting bag from the back bedroom and brought it down to the living room, before lifting out the remaining two balls of red wool along with the sweater pattern she'd already knitted six times. She then removed the No. 6 knitting needles in the bag, cast on several stitches and started to knit. She could almost make a small sweater in her sleep by now. "Miss Kershaw would never have believed it!" Jenny couldn't help thinking as she smiled.

After watching an episode of Dr Who, followed the X Factor, Jenny yawned and put the half-completed small tunic into Auntie Sue's small bag, ready for finishing in the next few days. "If there'd been a decent movie on, I might have stayed up longer, but I'll call it a day and head for bed," she decided.

Later on, before drifting off to sleep, Jenny prayed that Dr Tan and Meula's family in the Philippines would be contactable and safe. She also planned to donate her latest small sweater to Dr Tan's appeal. Some small child might benefit, just like six other young kids had done.

On the following Monday morning, while Dr Tan was standing in the Reception area of the Health Centre, Jenny thought it was the right time to approach him. "Dr Tan," she said, "I met your sister Meula at Sunnyside House at the weekend and was very sorry to hear about the typhoon in the Philippines where your family live."

Dr Tan responded, "Thanks, Jenny. I phoned my brother Arturo yesterday via an emergency government hotline and he told me that most of the villages on the island have been wiped out, with several hundred people still feared dead or missing. I'm not sure if all my relatives are dead or alive and I just want to get back home as soon as possible to share my medical skills wherever I can."

"When do you think you'll get back?" Jenny asked.

Dr Tan replied, "I'm hoping to leave next Friday. I've got a British Airways ticket from London to Bangkok in Thailand, plus a connecting flight from Bangkok to Manila on the Philippines mainland. I've already been given donated bandages, dressings and a host of small surgical instruments from my medical colleagues and will fill my extra baggage allowance with lots of children's clothes. None will be wasted. I'm planning to set up a small emergency clinic in Vanuatu to treat a range of survivors and been offered Special Leave from work for at least a month."

"Dr Tan," Jenny continued, "I've completed a small red sweater for your appeal and would be happy to assist with any further fundraising needs when you return. I'll be remembering you when you're away." Jenny felt privileged to offer her now completed small red sweater to Dr Tan's appeal.

On the following Friday afternoon, when Jenny returned to the Health Centre after finishing her visits for the day, she noticed a printed notice on the Reception desk. It read, "Dr Tan's clinics are cancelled until further notice." He would be helping to save many lives on the island of Vanuatu, on the other side of the world…

CHAPTER SEVENTEEN

RICO'S STORY (THE PHILIPPINES)

"Come on, Rico. Run! There's no time to lose. If you don't hurry up, you'll not make it to the shelter," Rico heard his mother, Jasmine, shouting as he ran as fast as he could from his home near the beach. Already the wind was getting stronger and huge waves had started to crash on the shore. Normally Rico loved hearing the sound of the waves, but tonight they looked and sounded different. He'd never seen them looking so big, and they were getting nearer every few minutes, dangerously close to his house. Rico breathlessly gasped, "I'm puffed! I think my lungs are going to burst!" as he climbed to the bamboo shelter at the top of the hill. His small sisters Mio and Blessica tried to keep up with him as they ran alongside, each holding one of his hands, whilst Jasmine followed close behind with grandmother, Che. There was no way that eighty-year-old Che had the energy to make it on her own, so Jasmine helped her to take one step at a time as they ascended the steep hill.

As Che slowly climbed, she stuttered, "These typhoons are getting more frequent and ferocious and I think this one brewing will be the worst one yet." Rico hoped she was wrong, but he knew typhoons were common in the Philippine Islands and were getting more powerful because of global warming.

"Do you think daddy will tie up our boat and make it up the hill in time?" Mio asked.

Jasmine replied, "I really hope he does, but if the waves come in any farther, he'll have to leave the boat behind." A lot of men on Vanuatu Island, like Rico's father Mindo, were fishermen, often out at sea for several hours each day, trying to catch enough fish for their own families plus extra to sell in the village. Jasmine usually cooked the fish that Mindo caught over a small charcoal fire but sometimes she dried it for later use if food might be scarce.

"I hope our house will be alright," muttered Blessica, "and I don't want the chickens to drown." Most of the island inhabitants like Rico's family lived near the beach in small wooden buildings on stilts with thatched roofs and outdoor steps leading to a small balcony. As the houses were raised, dried rice could also be stored underneath. Most of the fishermen's families ate rice every day, but if they made a good catch of fish they'd eat that too.

Most of the village neighbours had already arrived at the shelter by the time Rico and the others made it up the hill. "Let's stay close together and see if we can find somewhere to sit, although there isn't much room and we could be here for hours," Jasmine quietly whispered as Rico glanced out the doorway and saw several trees violently swaying from side to side. Normally Vanuatu Island was beautiful with lots of palm trees and blue tropical lagoons near the shore, but today it wasn't so lovely. In fact, it was starting to look like a nightmare, as rubbish began to whirl all over the place.

Jasmine quickly spotted a small space in a corner. "Quick everyone, sit down over here as it might be quieter and well away from the door." Rico and the others sat down, just as the wind got fiercer outside and heavy rain started to fall.

A few moments later a tired and breathless Mindo appeared. He was overjoyed his family had made it to the shelter, but told them, "I tried to tie our boat to a large tree, but suddenly I had to run to higher ground as huge waves, about twenty feet high, started crashing onto the beach."

At this stage the shelter began to get noisy as small babies started to cry and adults whispered about what might happen to their homes and crops. Che listened to the conversations then gently spoke. "I remember a huge typhoon when I was a little girl, when lots of houses were badly damaged and some fishermen were washed out to sea. The whole village got a brief warning, but some fishermen wouldn't leave their boats and left it too late to get away from the waves." Che shared a little more information about other tropical storms then added, "I think this one's going to be worse as I've never seen the waves so big or the wind blow up so quickly."

Rico and the others pretended not to hear, but knew Che was probably right, as she'd been around a long time and had lots of life experience. Rico had been brought up to always respect older people and he'd a lot of affection for Grandmother Che. He just hoped that her typhoon predictions were wrong!

"I wish this was all over," muttered Jasmine, as the wind started to wail, the shelter rocked from side to side and torrential rain beat onto the thatched roof. The only electric bulb also went out as the island power lines must have been damaged. "Don't worry, I've brought a torch," a voice shouted, but it didn't give out much light.

About twenty minutes later and without warning, an enormous moaning sound came from outside and the shelter roof blew off. Everyone was terrified. No one could escape the pounding rain and lashing wind and even the small babies in their parents' arms got soaked. Not even Che or the other villagers around her age had experienced such a ferocious storm before.

Various voices shouted out, "Help, my watch has stopped working." "My clothes are drenched." "My torch won't light up anymore as the batteries are ruined." There was nothing anything anyone could do about the damage, so they just had to ride out the storm. The adults tried their best to protect the children as some of the little ones began to fall asleep.

Several hours later, the howling wind died down and the rain eased off as Rico gazed up into the sky through the hole where the shelter roof had been and noticed a few stars still covered by hazy clouds. Mio, who'd almost fallen asleep, asked Jasmine, "When will it be morning? I want to go home." Jasmine hardly knew what to reply, as she was exhausted and fearful herself.

About another half hour later, the morning dawn broke through.

Mindo and a few other men slowly stood up and walked over to what had been the shelter doorway, now pummelled to bits by the wind. He stared down the hill with an air of sadness then suggested, "Let's walk down to the shore to see what remains of our homes." Slowly Mindo led his neighbours down the hill towards their former houses, with nearly all of them wrecked by the huge typhoon. Rico was horrified by all the damage.

"Our chickens have been drowned and all our things have been washed away in the tide," he said, almost choking on his words as he looked at what used to be his house. There was hardly anything left except a pile of broken wood, shattered glass and bits of twisted metal on the ground. Jasmine quietly wept as she carried Blessica in a small cloth sling on her back and tightly held onto Mio by the hand. Grandmother Che slowly followed behind but had to sit down on a large stone to rest, shattered by the horrors of the worst typhoon she'd ever seen.

It didn't take long to find Mindo's fishing boat, battered against the rocks and with a huge hole in the hull. "I don't think our boat will float anymore," Rico said as his father sadly nodded. Jasmine spotted the remains of her small charcoal stove, but it was wrecked as well. Lots of the other villagers were in the same situation and really didn't know what to do next.

After a short while, as Mindo and Rico started to gather some small fish that had been washed ashore, they heard Danilo, one of their neighbours call out, "Could you use a small bag of charcoal that I brought to the shelter last night?"

Mindo replied, "We certainly could. I could light a fire by rubbing stones together then put some of your charcoal on top. At least that means we'll be able to cook." Mindo and Jasmine walked their children away from the beach to a sheltered spot under the remains of a palm tree, then managed to light a small fire. Jasmine began to cook some of the fish on top of the fire, while Rico and his little sisters searched for fruit that had fallen from the trees.

Suddenly one of Rico's uncles appeared, holding onto Grandmother Che. "Grandmother can come and stay at my village for a while, as it wasn't as badly damaged as yours. I can help her to manage the steps outside my house as it's still standing on its stilts and didn't get flooded."

Mindo and Jasmine appreciated this kind offer. "We'll be glad to have Grandmother Che back very soon, but looking after her in your village would be much safer for her, too," Jasmine had to admit.

As the adults talked, Rico was shocked to see lots of his neighbours with bad cuts or broken limbs, some using fallen branches as walking sticks and others being carried on wooden planks from damaged houses. Many small children were also walking around barefoot, looking lost and searching for their parents. "Everyone looks really tired and dazed," Rico thought.

A short while later, some unfamiliar people arrived wearing T shirts and yellow plastic vests with small badges on the front. "I wish I could read what the badges say, but I don't know enough words at the moment," Rico muttered, as he knew he'd not be back at school for a very long time. These visitors were aid workers and most of them were lifting large boxes or bags from a truck. In no time they began to give out food, bottled water, blankets and clothing, while some of them set up a large tent for the injured near to the base of the hill and well away from the shore. "I'm glad none of my family needs to go to that tent," Rico thought to himself as his tummy rumbled with hunger.

The next few days passed in a blur. Mindo and some of the other men made simple homes from damaged trees with large fallen palm leaves for the canopy roofs, whilst Rico and Mio collected wild berries, fruit and small fish that were washed onto the beach. Jasmine queued every day to get clean bottled water for all the family, especially for Blessica, who was still quite small and at risk of dehydration. Rico also kept a look out for any unfamiliar adults as Jasmine had warned him, "There might be child traffickers about who want to take children away to places like Thailand to work them as slaves. The orphaned boys and girls are especially at risk."

Jasmine and Mindo always tried their best to protect their young family but were worried one morning when some strange people appeared and began to walk around the damaged village, staring at the children. One of Grandmother Che's cousins had been lured away from her village after a previous typhoon and never returned.

Another week later, a large jeep arrived at the devastated village and parked near the hill where the shelter had stood. More aid workers stepped out of the vehicle along with some government officials from Port Vila, the capital city. These people had brought lots more boxes of food and clothes with them, plus bottled water and hygiene kits.

Rico recognised one of the faces and said to Mio who stood beside him, "I think that's the nice doctor who came to our village last year. I remember he gave me an injection." Rico knew he'd probably come back to help the injured and to give more injections to prevent a nasty disease. Two aid workers from the jeep, who were carrying several boxes and a bag, walked over to Jasmine, Mindo and Blessica, who were sheltering under a tree in the sun, and offered them a food parcel, a blanket, a fishing net, cooking utensils and a small spade. Rico and Mio joined the rest of the family as one of the ladies opened another large bag and lifted out two small T shirts which she gave to Jasmine for Mio and Blessica.

"I've the very thing that'll fit you," she then said as she dipped back into the bag and pulled out a lovely sweater for Rico. "Dr Tan, who's here today, brought this from Northern Ireland and he's going to set up a new clinic in the village. You might have seen him when he came last year." Rico was thrilled to get the new sweater. The stitches were simple and neat, and it looked nicer than the sweater he'd worn when he helped his father to fish before the typhoon.

The Vanuatu islanders, like Rico's family, were resourceful people who'd faced many storms before, and with outside help, would soon have their homes rebuilt and boats repaired. Rico planned to wear his new sweater when he got back to helping Mindo on a new boat and muttered, "I just hope there'll not be any more typhoons in Vanuatu for a very long time!"

CHAPTER EIGHTEEN

JENNY GOES TO HAITI

Dr Tan set his pen down on the desk in front then leaned over onto his elbows. "Jenny, a little boy called Rico got your red tunic and I can't begin to tell you how much he loved it. Most of the people in his village lost their homes in the typhoon and have had to start from scratch again. I only got to spend two weeks in the Philippines last month but was able to treat a number of people who'd been injured in the violent storm. Most had nasty cuts from broken wood or fractured limbs from falling trees. I also did some first aid training with local community leaders and gave lots of vaccinations."

"I'm glad you were able to help many people after the typhoon, Dr Tan, and I'm sure they valued your advice," responded Jenny. "The niece of a friend recently completed her medical elective in Sudan and told me about your volunteering work after one of your student lectures in Queens University. You've certainly inspired young medical students like her to take a compassionate interest in disaster work themselves."

"Thanks, Jenny," Dr Tan responded. "I really appreciated the medical students who fundraised for the Philippine Hospitals' Appeal last year. They've all got the makings of becoming great doctors! Of course, I'm delighted by your own news, Jenny, as I really hoped someone from the Health Centre would volunteer to go to Haiti. That country got hit hard by an earthquake a couple of years ago, and, of course, by the recent Hurricane Matthew. I know you'll be a great help there and no doubt you're relieved that your typhoid jab today is the last injection you'll need before you go. Head home now and have a restful night but remember to start your anti-malarial tablets next Tuesday, two days before you leave." Jenny had hardly felt

Dr Tan's injection needle piercing her skin and was really glad she could put her jacket back on and leave the surgery, as she'd removed it to get her typhoid injection. She could hardly believe she'd responded to the following notice on the Staff Health Centre bulletin board:

Volunteer Nurses required for clinic in Haiti
Band 3–8 grades.
Availability required for 3–6 week period.
To assist at vaccination clinic in Port-au-Prince and in resettlement camps, as required.
Must have updated UK Professional Registration.
Travel Clinic can offer advice on necessary inoculations. Knowledge of French advisable but not essential.
Please contact Human Resources Department for further details.

As Jenny had scanned this advertisement, images of Auntie Sue in Vietnam and of Tracey in Sudan came into her mind, as a question played on her conscience, "Why not volunteer for a trip like this yourself?" She had to admit she was in pretty good health, had no dependent children, animals or elderly parents, and no husband waiting at home, which made her give a low sigh. She also knew she'd a lot of nursing skills to offer like completing complex dressings, prescribing treatment for lots of common ailments and giving vaccinations, which would be particularly useful as a recent cholera outbreak had started to spread.

Later that day, Jenny had contacted the Human Resources Department and was advised, "A Volunteer Application form will be in the post by tomorrow. Please return your completed form by the closing date in one week's time."

Four weeks on, Jenny had managed to be granted two weeks' unpaid leave and an extra two weeks' annual leave. She'd got her suitcase packed, completed her vaccinations and gathered up some nursing supplies. Jenny was ready for Haiti…

In Haiti

Jenny couldn't believe the amount of devastation she saw when she arrived at Port-au-Prince. She quickly noticed several cracks in the walls of the airport terminal building and lots of potholes on the roads as she travelled in a crowded taxi to her base at one of the large resettlement camps outside Port-au-Prince. "Gosh, look at all those homes reduced to rubble," Jenny couldn't help thinking. "Some of them probably have family members still buried underneath."

As Jenny arrived at the resettlement camp, she couldn't believe the number of tents set up for families to live, giving them a basic level of shelter and the opportunity for a "near normal" life after their recent loss.

Very quickly she met her fellow volunteers. One of them, called Randy, had come from the USA. "I'm from Alabama and came here when I heard about the devastation," he shared with Jenny. "I graduated from med school last year and did some volunteering in Peru and North East Brazil the year before." Jenny immediately thought she'd enjoy working along with Randy. She also felt an immediate bond with Greta from Germany, who'd a kind smile.

Greta shared with Jenny, "I come from Berlin and plan to be here for four months. My husband recently died, and I thought this would be a chance for me to heal while I try to help heal others. At home I work as a nurse but am also a qualified midwife." This encouraged Jenny herself.

Most of the camp volunteers came from the USA, but others represented Japan, France, Australia, Ireland and the UK, plus Germany, where Greta was from, all there to share their medical skills and support.

Every day was busy at the camp. "Do you think we're going to be worked hard today?" Jenny asked Greta during her second week, as they walked from their volunteer accommodation tent to the large prefabricated multi-purpose hall in centre of the camp.

"Yes, we certainly will be. It's a Monday, so there'll be vaccinations plus a mother and baby clinic this morning, then an HIV support group this afternoon. In the evening the hall will be used as a youth club and a place for adults to meet. In fact, I think it's used every evening."

Jenny was impressed by how all available space was well used. "It's great the children have got two old buses as temporary school classrooms, the red one for children under seven and the other green one for older kids up to thirteen." Greta had to agree with her as she showed Jenny another nearby wooden building that was used as a church, plus a small open fronted shop and a water pump standing nearby.

It was a busy morning. Several mothers with babies came for advice on nutrition plus sixty children were given cholera vaccinations as the disease was still a risk in the camp. Jenny really felt sorry for all the Haitian people who'd lost someone close through the recent disasters, with many finding it hard to express their grief. "Maybe I could help to set up a trauma support group," Jenny discussed with Randy later in the morning, when he arrived at the hall to help complete the vaccination session.

One little girl especially touched Jenny's heart when she arrived for her jab. She told Jenny her name was Helene and that her home had been destroyed by the recent hurricane floods, despite getting rebuilt after the earthquake two years before. She shared, "I was getting ready to go to school when I heard a loud whooshing noise outside. My mum, Estelle was cooking some small bananas for breakfast when she suddenly shouted at me to get out of the house quickly as the local riverbank had burst its banks. I grabbed my school bag while my mother kept holding onto her only pan, then we both ran out of the house. We were really frightened and there wasn't time to lose."

Helene wanted to go back for their small pet dog, but Estelle stopped her and had kept saying, "There isn't time. We must keep going. We'll get stuck in the flood if we don't move quickly." Jenny understood that but Helene continued, "We ran towards a big community hall near our home with lots of neighbours who carried baskets of goods on their heads or rolls of bedding under their arms. By the time we'd almost got there it was hard to escape the flood. I couldn't run very fast and got sucked into the flowing water as the torrential rain came down and lightning crashed over my head. I tried to hold onto my mother's hand, but my fingers loosened, and I had to let go. Then I dropped my schoolbag and it got washed away."

Jenny felt sorry for the little girl as she must have been terrified and kept listening as she told her story.

"Eventually, a big helicopter came. People wearing uniforms jumped out of it with parachutes attached to their bodies that opened in the air. All of them landed on trees, with their parachutes spreading over the branches. More men, wearing the same uniforms, then arrived in small rowing boats and coaxed everyone in the crowd to get into a boat, before rowing all of us to the community hall. By the time my mother and I got there, the whole ground floor was covered in water. We found a safe place on the first floor where we couldn't drown and anyway, there was nowhere else to go. We were just really glad to be safe."

Helene's family now lived in a tent as a temporary home with extra emergency cooking pots, food and water. Her father, brother and two sisters also survived the hurricane as they were staying with other relatives on the morning the flooding began. It was going to be a tough job for each of them to keep healthy and to start their lives again; that's why Helene had come to the camp clinic to get her vaccination. Jenny was touched by her story and just glad she could do something practical to halt a deadly virus that could make life even more dangerous for Helene and the other camp survivors.

In no time, it was Jenny's last week in Haiti and the chance to share her nursing skills at a different clinic in a town southwest of Port-au-Prince called Jacmel. Greta, Randy and Jenny had enjoyed working together and couldn't believe it was nearly time for Jenny to return home to Northern Ireland.

"We'll miss you, Jenny," said Randy. "You've been a great help with giving vaccinations and I know lots of our patients really liked you. Let me help you lift those boxes of supplies into the back of the van." Randy helped Jenny to load boxes of syringes and dressings into the back of a small minivan as Greta got into the front beside the driver. The van slowly weaved through heavy traffic towards the clinic, crossing a bridge over one of the main rivers in the city.

As Jenny glanced out the window she turned and spoke to Randy. "I see this area must have been badly hit by the earthquake and the recent floods." Randy nodded in agreement as the driver tried to negotiate several potholes on the road.

A few moments later Greta turned around in the front seat and exclaimed, "Just look at that man over there. He seems to be selling tablets from a large hat on his head!" Jenny gave a slight giggle as she thought it looked slightly comical, but knew this was probably his main livelihood. Greta continued, "He's probably done some pharmacy training in the USA. No doubt he's got a lot more knowledge in making all sorts of lotions and potions than we have!"

Jenny responded, "You're right, Greta. He's the sort of person we might need at our clinic!" As Jenny's own Dad still worked as a pharmacist, she knew how challenging this kind of job could be, especially in a place where money and resources were scarce.

As the minivan continued along the narrow, busy streets Jenny noticed many traders on the roadsides, selling everything from soap and candles to batteries, jewellery and soft drinks. Some of the stallholders displayed a range of clothes and shoes. Others sold small bread sticks made from water and flour.

Jenny turned to Greta as she spotted several school children walking quickly along some of the damaged pavements and said, "I think those kids are beautifully clean and well-presented, especially as it must be very hard for their mothers or carers to wash their white blouses and shirts in small temporary shelters. I think many of the girls look really pretty with their plaited locks and tiny beads in their hair." Greta heartily responded as she attempted to secure the pins at the crown of her head.

It wasn't long before the minivan pulled up outside a large whitewashed hall with a small painted sign at the doorway written in French Creole and English. It simply stated, "Clinic today." Randy explained, "This building is hired out by a local church to a range of charities each week, including small self-help groups that give financial and practical help to many folks in Jacmel. It's great we're getting the chance to use it today."

After Jenny, Greta and Randy climbed out of the minivan, they quickly walked around to the rear door and lifted out their boxes of medical supplies before carrying them into the hall where about a hundred women and small babies were already waiting for the clinic to start.

In no time, everything was unpacked, and the clinic got underway. Jenny and Greta agreed to cover the main vaccinations while Ricky dealt with any complex cases that arrived. It looked like a busy afternoon ahead!

When four o'clock eventually came, Jenny and Greta felt really exhausted and were keen to start clearing up. "I'll put the spare syringes in these bags, if you'd make sure all the unused vaccines are back in the cool box for later use." Jenny suggested to Greta.

"No problem, Greta replied. "I can't believe we carried out over a hundred and twenty jabs this afternoon. I believe Randy dealt with several small toddlers who showed signs of cholera. It's sad the virus still seems to be spreading after the recent hurricane floods." This made Jenny think of Helena, who she'd met at one of her earlier vaccination clinics, and hoped her young brother and sisters were doing okay.

Suddenly and without warning, Jenny began to feel dizzy. The ground seemed to start shaking and her body swayed from side to side, making her lose control. A few seconds later a huge crack appeared on a nearby wall followed by a further large crack on the floor. Panic broke out as adults and children started to scream and ran towards the exit door. Others seemed too frightened to move. Pieces of the ceiling roof fell onto Jenny's head whilst a light fitting crashed to the ground and landed by her foot. Jenny tried to sit up then remembered a piece of advice from her training preparation course – "Run towards the nearest door." If this was an earthquake tremor, that's what she needed to do. Jenny called out, "Greta, where are you? Where's Randy?" before, and without warning, a large piece of concrete smashed on top of her left leg. Then Jenny fainted with the pain...

CHAPTER NINETEEN

TRAGEDY IN HAITI

Jenny blinked her eyes as a strong shaft of light beamed through the window. "Where am I? When did I get here?" she called out in panic as she slowly woke up from a deep sleep. She soon realised she was in a hospital ward with several other patients around her and felt someone gently removing a blood pressure cuff from her arm. As she lifted her head off her pillow and glanced down the bed, Jenny noticed her left foot and ankle covered by a large plaster cast which was suspended by a small pulley attached to a frame. A shocked Jenny cried out, "I can't move my leg and my ankle hurts," as the young nurse who'd been checking her blood pressure tried to comfort her and offered her some bottled water to sip. Jenny took a few sips of water then gently sank back onto the bed.

For a short while Jenny stared quietly at the ceiling while disturbing images seemed to float through her head. She imagined she was lying under a huge pile of concrete rubble with her hands pinned to her sides and a large broken slab crushing her chest. In the darkness she could hear loud crashing noises and lots of voices shouting for help, some of them in Creole French, the main spoken language of Haiti.

Jenny moaned softly as further images replayed in her brain. This time she felt someone's arms pulling her out of the rubble then several hands lifting her onto a stretcher. Her rescuers seemed to be wearing yellow vests, some with a NYFP badge on the front. Jenny knew this stood for the "New York Fire Department" because Steve had already told her this. Most of the rescuers' voices sounded American or Creole French, but one had a Northern Irish accent not unlike Jenny's own...

A few minutes later, Jenny lifted her head off the pillow as a doctor, who was wearing a white coat, arrived and introduced himself. "Good afternoon, I'm Dr Chen, the current Registrar on Ward 10. I understand your name is Jenny, and that you were admitted to this hospital three days ago after your rescue from a clinic in Jacmel. You have a complex lower limb fracture, although I expected your level of injury to be more severe. Your heart rate and temperature are now at satisfactory levels, but your ankle joint is unlikely to heal for some time."

Jenny tried to keep focusing her eyes on Dr Chen as he moved to the side of the bed to share more information. "Your ankle fracture will require complete rest with no weight-bearing for several weeks, then you will have therapy to get you stepping and walking again. Your Travel Insurance Company will be able to arrange an Air Ambulance to assist your return home after I deem you medically fit to travel."

Dr Chen leaned forward to review the plaster cast on Jenny's ankle as she noticed several patients moving about in a nearby corridor with walking sticks or in wheelchairs. The doctor adjusted the small pulley attached to the frame over Jenny's leg then signed a chart at the end of her bed, before announcing, "I'll review your fracture in two days' time. I need to leave you now to attend another patient." As Jenny watched Dr Chen depart, she suddenly heard another voice at the side of the bed, which sounded American and vaguely familiar.

"Jenny, I've been trying to find you over the past three days and saw your name on one of the hospital survivor lists this morning. None of the other clinic volunteers knew if you'd been rescued since the earthquake. I'm so glad you're here."

Jenny slowly pushed herself up onto her elbows and gazed at the face in front. "Oh Randy, it's you! I'm still not sure how I got here. I vaguely remember packing up supplies at our clinic in Jacmel when the floor started to move under my feet, and I couldn't stand anymore." Jenny noticed Randy had a nasty cut on his forehead, but he continued to speak.

"I thought I'd better check the state of you, Jenny. Sorry to see the damage to your ankle but it should heal pretty soon. I guess you could say we're both survivors!" As Jenny scanned the injuries of several other patients on the ward, she agreed it was a miracle they'd both been spared.

"What happened to Greta?" Jenny then asked as her mind began to focus more clearly.

Randy replied, "I heard Greta wasn't actually hurt but is very traumatised by the quake. She's staying with some German volunteer friends in a Red Cross temporary hostel on the main road between Port-au-Prince and Jacmel Districts." Jenny was pleased to hear Greta didn't have any serious injuries and had the support of her German friends.

Randy chatted on for another few minutes before Jenny's eyelids began to get heavy and she could no longer stay awake…

A few hours later, Jenny re-opened her eyes and noticed a small electric light bulb glowing from the ceiling above, whilst she looked through the windows and saw it was almost dark outside. A young Haitian nurse returned to check her blood pressure and said, "A visitor arrived at the ward about an hour ago and asked to speak to you, but I told him you were sleeping. I believe he might have assisted in your rescue operation." The nurse continued, "As he's still here, would you care to speak to him now?"

Jenny couldn't work out who the visitor might be but replied, "I'll agree to meet him but my hair's a real mess and I'm hardly awake!"

The young nurse gently laughed as she placed a pillow behind Jenny's head to help her sit up, and said, "I wouldn't fret about your hair, Jenny. You've come through a lot in the past few days and I'm sure your visitor will understand." A few minutes later, after the nurse returned to her office, a young gentleman appeared at the entrance of the ward and made his way towards Jenny. On approaching the bed, Jenny couldn't help thinking his lean muscular frame reminded her of Steve, although unlike Steve, he had fair hair and blue eyes.

"Hi Jenny, my name's Mike," the visitor uttered as he leaned forward to shake Jenny's hand. "I just wanted to call by and check your progress." Jenny noticed a NYFD badge on his shirt as he continued, "I arrived in Haiti earlier this week and have been involved with the earthquake recovery operation, including in Jacmel District three days ago. Several bodies were recovered in the area that day but by mid-afternoon it looked unlikely that further survivors would be found. As I prepared to leave the site of a former building that had been reduced to rubble, I thought I heard a faint voice and decided to keep searching with a sniffer dog's help. That's when I located you and assisted to lift you from the fallen debris and onto a stretcher."

Jenny was astounded and lost for words. After a few moments, she responded. "Mike, I can't thank you enough for what you've done for me. Without your heroic efforts, I might have lost my leg or even my life beneath that rubble."

"No problem, Jenny," replied Mike. "That's what I was trained for. To act fast, to show courage and to be there when others need me. You must have been terrified while you waited for help."

Jenny sighed as she replied, "I don't remember much, but I think I called out a few times and also kept praying that someone would find me. My prayers were certainly heard. I also kept thinking about a little girl in Nepal who'd survived a recent earthquake herself. If she could make it, and she did, then so could I."

"I guess that must have been the huge earthquake that hit central Nepal earlier this year," Mike responded. "Some friends of mine were also there at the time."

Jenny confirmed it was, then posed a question to Mike. "Are you from Northern Ireland by any chance? I recognised your accent, but you obviously work in New York now, after looking at your badge."

"Gosh, Jenny, you're observant," Mike replied. "I used to live and work in Northern Ireland but moved to the States eighteen months ago to join the New York Fire Department. I guess I needed some time away to heal from the past myself..."

Jenny realized there must have been some troubling matter but didn't want to pry. "I'm sure it was difficult to leave your family behind," she quietly stated before Mike replied with a small hesitant sigh.

"Jenny, sometimes you've got to make a new start. I faced a terrible loss before I came to New York, but now I'm glad I made the move and love being based in Manhattan. As I've firefighter skills, I also decided to volunteer for search and rescue missions after natural disasters. I've already been in Central and South America, and now of course, I'm here. Four of my colleagues recently completed disaster response volunteering at a Philippine island called Vanuatu, which I believe was struck by a large typhoon. I guess you wouldn't know where that was, Jenny."

Jenny gave a faint smile as she knew only too well but didn't want to share that straight away. It was hard not to think about little Rico and the other islanders who'd lost so much in the violent typhoon.

As Jenny stretched and tried to sit up a bit more, Mike asked, "Jenny, would you by any chance have had a husband called Steve O'Neill?"

"Yes," Jenny slowly replied, "I did." Mike took a deep breath and spoke again. "Jenny, I don't think you're a stranger to pain yourself. I used to work with your husband Steve as part of Blue Watch within the Belfast Central Fire Department. He's the most courageous and caring guy I've ever met."

Mike tried to stifle a choke as he continued. "I was on duty with Steve on the day he died. No doubt you know our Watch was called out about nine o'clock that evening to deal with a vicious fire on the fifth floor of a multi-storey tower block, accidentally caused by a burning chip pan. A young mother and her three small children were trapped inside their apartment, which was at the source of the fire. The mother managed to escape by jumping from a windowsill onto a tarpaulin that had been set up in the car park below whilst her seven-year-old son and five-year-old daughter were located and carried outside. However, another child, a three-year-old girl, was still inside the tower and by now the heat from the fire had shattered all the windows on the south side of the building and flames had begun to reach the top floor."

Jenny could hardly believe what she was hearing. Mike continued, "At that point, Steve re-entered the building to rescue the three-year-old child. He managed to locate her in a bedroom before passing her through a broken window to waiting colleagues outside, who then carried her to safety. I believe she sustained some second degree burns but has since recovered well."

Mike took another breath before he spoke again. "The main staircase in the tower block then started to collapse as Steve ran towards the ground floor. We tried to reach him but were beaten back by toxic smoke as the whole ground floor was now ablaze. There was nothing we could do to save him. I can't tell you how thankful I was to have had a colleague like Steve. He was a real inspiration to the rest of us. I knew he'd a wife, but of course, I never got the chance to meet you. I can see he had good taste ..."

Jenny gave a faint smile as she fought back tears. "Thanks, Mike," she quietly replied. "You'll never know how much that information means to me. I never knew exactly what happened to Steve on the night he died, and was always too shocked or sad to ask for the details. Thanks for sharing them with me."

"Jenny," Mike then whispered, "I can understand some of your pain. Perhaps I ran away to America to escape my own grief. I haven't quite decided yet if I'm going to stay in the States, although I've an older brother in Boston. I don't get much time to meet my American neighbours as being a firefighter means lots of late nights and anti-social hours, but of course, you'd know all about that."

"I certainly do," Jenny responded with a smile.

Mike paused then added, "I hope your ankle heals real fast, Jenny, and that you'll soon be back to the woman you were. I believe you work as a nurse back home and were doing some volunteering work when the earthquake struck. I must say I admire you for that. No doubt, you've other interests, too."

Jenny didn't waste time in telling Mike about her new knitting hobby, including the locations where her little sweaters ended up. She also told him about her late Auntie Sue and her volunteering work as a nurse. Mike was impressed. "That sounds like a worthwhile hobby that was started by your Aunt. In fact, I know my NYFP colleagues who went to Vanuatu gave out some small sweaters and cardigans as part of the recovery operation. I'm glad one of your little sweaters got there, too. I have to admit I usually just play a little golf or attend an ice hockey match on my rare days off."

After chatting for a short while longer, Jenny began to feel drowsy again and whispered in a small, croaky voice. "I wish you well after all you've been through yourself, Mike. I guess you're right about needing to move on."

In no time Jenny fell back to sleep.

CHAPTER TWENTY

JENNY COMES HOME

Jenny hobbled towards the TV with a crutch in one hand and a duster in the other, then scanned her eyes across the room. "This place is rather dusty and if Auntie Sue were here, she'd be saying the room needs a good clean!" Jenny had to admit to herself. At least there was an excuse for the dust as she'd been covering extra shifts at work before leaving for Haiti as well as being away for longer than expected. At least she only needed one crutch now as her left ankle was healing well and she could now walk safely about the house, including using the stairs.

"I'd better make a start. Heavier jobs can wait until I've a bit more get up and go!" Jenny muttered as she spotted a pile of old magazines and a small cardboard box on the floor. "I can't remember what I put in that box," Jenny couldn't help thinking, but it didn't look too heavy, so she decided to postpone the dusting and to check through the box instead.

Jenny managed to carry the box over to an armchair and set it on her knee before blowing off a layer of dust and opening the lid. A pile of envelopes, several shopping receipts and some bills quickly appeared as well as her old passport which she'd replaced before going to Haiti. As she flicked through these items, Jenny noticed two airmail letters, one with a Sudanese stamp and another from Sierra Leone. "I'm so glad I kept these," Jenny muttered to herself as she began to read the two letters. One was a note from Tracey during her placement in Sudan who'd mentioned little Yaya receiving Jenny's sweater and the other was from Carley in Sierra Leone, writing about Nouhou's recovery from Ebola.

As Jenny returned the airmail letters to the cardboard box she stopped to ponder for a moment. "It's great Auntie Sue's old knitting pattern was a link between these little kids on the African continent, and I can't believe I've actually knitted seven wee sweaters that have crossed borders around the globe!"

Just the weekend before she'd met Andy outside the Sports Centre and he'd told her more details about Parbati. Apparently, she'd returned to her village and was now living with her family in a newly constructed house. Jenny had also gone to Mike and Pearl's on Friday evening for supper when Mike mentioned he was returning to Calais in the autumn with further donated items for Syrian refugee families, like Jamirah's.

Jenny had also bumped into Robert at the Post Office when she'd called in to buy stamps. He reported he still enjoyed his new job including regular overland journeys to Romania and hoped to check on little Stefan and his brother during his next trip.

"It's great my little sweaters have reached all these kids," Jenny whispered to herself. "Of course, I also heard about José." She'd got more information about the Mexico Team when she'd had lunch at Ricky and Lisa's on Sunday. Fifty children had attended the Football Academy and each team member had completed the project they'd wanted to support. It was uplifting to hear what each had achieved in such a short time, and great that they were able to distribute the donated goods they'd brought in their luggage! Apparently, a little boy called José had received Jenny's red sweater! Dr Tan also paid a visit during the week to check Jenny's medical progress and shared details about his recent Trip to Vanuatu Island, including the mention of a boy called Rico who'd also received one of Jenny's knits! As Dr Tan hoped to return to the island in a few months' time he was likely to meet Rico and his family again as Rico's grandmother often came to one of his clinics for treatment. As Jenny then brought her thoughts back to the box on her knee she decided to rummage some more. "Might be something of interest in here," she thought as her fingers suddenly felt an envelope with something hard inside. Jenny gently lifted out the envelope, peeled back the flap and looked inside. A tear rolled down her cheek as she realised it was the small identity badge that Steve had often worn on his firefighter jacket, but not on the night he'd died, as his jacket had been left at the station. As Jenny slowly placed the badge back into the envelope she couldn't help thinking, "This is another bit of Steve that I'll never give away." For the meantime, she returned the badge to the box and closed the lid.

As Jenny glanced around the room again, she noticed Auntie Sue's small red knitting bag lying by the side of the sofa with two new balls of wool inside. Carole had called the day before and left the wool as a gift with the order, "Time to do more knitting!" Jenny knew Carole was right. Seven small children had already benefitted from her knitting skills and there could potentially be more! Making the small sweaters had been therapy for herself and a great way to resurrect her knitting skills, despite what Miss Kershaw had believed about her limited knitting talents!

Jenny quickly decided to postpone her dusting for another few minutes as she walked over to the sofa and lifted up the knitting bag. Just as she began to pull out a ball of wool, she heard the doorbell ring...

"I'm not expecting anyone," Jenny thought as she glanced at her watch, which showed two minutes past three. She quickly squeezed the ball of wool back into the bag, slowly stood up then walked to the front door with her crutch. As she turned the key to open the door Jenny couldn't believe what she saw. A tall male figure with fair hair and blue eyes stood on the doorstep, casually dressed in a pair of blue jeans and checked shirt. He also carried a small blue rucksack on his back.

"Mike, what are you doing here?" Jenny blurted out, while she tried to hide a broad smile.

Mike responded with a slight grin himself. "I've decided to come home for a while. The Fire Service Chief thought I looked pretty shattered when I returned to New York and ordered me to take a few months off. His Travel Agent wife also booked me on a cheap flight to Dublin, so I can't complain. I'm here now and going nowhere fast!"

Jenny was aware that she was blushing slightly as she opened the door a bit further and welcomed Mike into her home. "Please feel free to come in, Mike. I don't want to leave you standing at the door. I was thinking about doing some knitting but wouldn't mind putting the kettle on for a quick cuppa instead. You're very welcome to join me!"

"Sounds a good offer!" Mike responded as he stepped through the door and followed Jenny up the hallway. When they reached the living room, Jenny invited Mike to sit down. "Mike, please make yourself at home while I go and sort coffee. No doubt you're tired." Jenny lifted up her crutch and headed for the kitchen as Mike sat down on the sofa and stretched out his legs, whilst noticing the small red knitting bag on the floor near his feet.

"I know Jenny knits little sweaters and it looks like she's starting another one now," Mike thought as a ball of red wool peeked from the opening of the bag.

As Mike surveyed the room, he noticed the black and white photo of a young nurse on the opposite wall. She wore a smart tunic dress, topped by a white starched apron and fastened by a black belt with a buckle around her waist. Her hair was also tied into a neat bun at the back of her head, covered by a white starched cap on her crown. "This young nurse looks very like Jenny and might be the Aunt she told me about in Haiti," Mike couldn't help thinking to himself.

As his gaze moved further along the wall, Mike quietly gasped as the face of his former colleague shone out from another photo. "How could I forget you, Steve?" he mumbled, as a tightness gripped his chest. "I still miss you every day. The whole of Blue Watch will never forget your courage and skill."

Just then, Jenny returned from the kitchen, carrying a steaming cup of coffee in one hand and her crutch in the other. "Mike, could I ask you to grab this from my hand? I don't want to let go of my crutch and am scared of spilling your drink," she uttered as Mike reached forward to lift the mug. "I've added milk but forgot if you take sugar," Jenny continued.

"No thanks, Jenny," Mike replied. "I'm sweet enough!"

"Oh, that's good," Jenny responded. "Better for your teeth. Maybe you should wait a few minutes to let your coffee cool down before you drink it."

"Good advice," Mike agreed. "You're a real gem going to the trouble to make this, especially when walking's still a bit of a challenge for you."

Jenny then left the room and returned a couple of minutes later with her own filled mug, then removed a couple of orange club biscuits from her pocket and handed one to Mike. "Sorry my catering's a bit rough and ready," she mumbled, "but I couldn't carry a plate as well as a mug! I'm still not too happy without a crutch in my hand, but one of these days I might be able to walk a bit further and faster!"

"That's the spirit, Jenny," Mike responded as he placed his drink onto the small coffee table in front. "You'll get there! You're a brave woman. I'll never forget your patience and resilience as you waited to be rescued from under the rubble."

"Thanks, Mike," Jenny said. "If it wasn't for your efforts, I might not be here at all apart from a leg that's still under repair."

"It was a privilege to do what I could," Mike stated. "I'm glad you're safely home now with an ankle that looks a lot less swollen than it did a couple of months ago. I just hope it's not too sore to walk on."

"No, it's not," replied Jenny. "It's a bit painful near the end of the day, but it's not as weak as it was. I'm not going back to work for a while, but the District Nursing service is hardly falling apart because I'm not there!"

"I'm not so sure about that, Jenny. It probably is!" interjected Mike with a chuckle. "No doubt your patients miss you, and I also think it's time you got back to your knitting! Your talents have certainly been reaching around the world from what I've heard!"

Jenny laughed before she posed another question. "What about your own plans, Mike, now that you're on leave yourself?"

He replied, "I'm not doing a lot at the moment. I bought a small apartment in the city centre before I left for New York, and it's been a great wee pad to come back to. I'm also keeping an eye on my folks who live off the Antrim Road and am doing the odd job for them, like tasks that need climbing up a ladder to complete. Nothing like making the best use of my firefighter training!"

Jenny and Mike continued to banter for a few minutes as they finished their coffee and biscuits before Mike leaned forward and reached for the small blue rucksack that he'd been carrying on his back. He opened the zip and pulled out a small parcel which was covered in sturdy brown paper. "I want to give you something that's meant a lot to me," Mike said with a slight hesitation as he handed the parcel to Jenny. "I know Steve would have wanted you to have this."

Jenny slowly opened the parcel's packaging and choked back a few tears as she realised the object inside was a firefighter's glove. The outer thermal cloth fabric seemed badly singed and two of the fingertips had obviously been burnt in a fire.

Mike explained, "This was one of the thermal gloves that Steve wore on the night of the Reaville Tower fire. His other glove was completely destroyed but the Hospital Accident & Emergency staff returned this one to out Fire Chief. He knew I was a good buddy of Steve's so passed it onto me. Jenny, after all you've been through yourself, I think you're the one who deserves to keep it now."

As Jenny gently stroked the glove in her hand and held it up to her face, she could smell a slight whiff of lingering smoke in the fabric. She then turned to Mike and said, "I can't thank you enough, I will treasure this for the rest of my life. I can't believe this glove covered Steve's strong hand as he tried to rescue others in the fire."

Jenny carefully placed the charred glove onto the coffee table as Mike removed another parcel from his rucksack.

"This is also something for yourself," Mike said. "You've been kind to others and also good to me. One good deed deserves another!"

Jenny couldn't help smiling as she slowly opened the New Look plastic bag and lifted out a beautiful red sweater.

"Mike, you're so thoughtful," she said. "I know I've knitted a few red sweaters, but I didn't think I'd ever receive one myself! It's just perfect and you've even got the right size. I love it!"

"Great," Mike said in response, "It'll soon be autumn and you might need something like this to keep warm! I wouldn't mind if you knitted me a jumper, but I'm not sure red's my colour!"

Jenny responded with a small giggle. "Just as well, Mike. I've only got two balls of red wool in my bag! Still, I like a challenge! When I'm a bit stronger I'll go into town and buy some more, but I'll need two free hands to carry the wool."

"I know you'll get there! Steve would be proud of you!" Mike had to admit. "By the way, Steve used to tell me that you enjoyed going to the movies and I'm rather fond of them myself. What about going to a movie tonight? There's a few good ones on at Yorkgate Cinema complex and if you'd like to join me, I could give you a lift and promise to get you home safely. I wouldn't mind a night out!"

Mike lifted Jenny's crutch from the floor and offered her his forearm to help her stand up, as he smiled and softly whispered, "Jenny, let's take a step into the future. You've plenty of time to do more knitting!"

Jenny looked up and couldn't help glancing at the photos of Auntie Sue and Steve on the wall. Both were smiling...

The author

Born and raised in Northern Ireland, Jacqui Davey
has been employed as an Occupational Therapist
by the NHS for over 35 years, and has volunteered
in overseas mission trips in Africa, Asia and the
Caribbean. She enjoys writing, baking, knitting
and a good book, as well as local walks, coffee
shop trips, and supporting her church community;
however, in light of a recent cancer diagnosis and
treatment, she has chosen to slow her life down.

The publisher

*He who stops
getting better
stops being good.*

This is the motto of novum publishing, and our focus
is on finding new manuscripts, publishing them and
offering long-term support to the authors.
Our publishing house was founded in 1997, and since
then it has become THE expert for new authors and
has won numerous awards.

**Our editorial team will peruse each manuscript
within a few weeks free of charge and without
obligation.**

You will find more information about
novum publishing and our books on the internet:

w w w . n o v u m - p u b l i s h i n g . c o . u k